The Apprentice

The Apprentice

—⋙—

A Thriller

Rick Pullen

ISBN 9780999491003
ISBN: 0999491008

A Blair House First Edition
Printed in USA

Fiction is fact distilled into truth.
—Edward Albee

For Cherie

Acknowledgements

Thanks to Jill Howard for your plot insights. You put a great twist on everything. Thanks to my editor Diane Krause. Your grammatical math skills (addition and subtraction), make me sound better than I am. Thank you to Kelsey Laye for your advice on medical issues. And Tish Carden, wow, your insights inspired this novel. Thanks for doing lunch and explaining your world.

Finally, thanks to Cherie for reading this over and over again, and for your insights about what works and what doesn't.

I

"Tish? Can you hear me?"

Damn it. What was with her? He stared at Tish through his view-finder, zooming in over the heads of the crowd. She was talking into her hand-held microphone in the far corner of the cavernous ballroom near the stage, but he could hear nothing through his headset.

At any minute, America would learn if Holly Crofton would become the first woman president in U.S. history. The story was huge. They needed to be ready.

Just a week ago, it didn't seem possible. Crofton and her running mate, Derrick Templeton, had lagged behind Republican Steve Berry by more than five percentage points. But now the room was abuzz with veiled murmurs of an upset. It was as if they were all watching a major league no-hitter. No one wanted to mention the word out loud for fear of jinxing the outcome.

Lording over the ballroom from large projection television screens at each side of the stage, CNN announced Florida for Crofton. The fuse of optimism was lit.

What a difference a few hours made. Earlier in the evening, a slow trickle of the faithful had filed through the ballroom doors, mingling with their forlorn cocktails in the half-filled room waiting hopelessly for a long-shot electoral reprieve.

Tom's adrenalin was pumped. He loved the rush of a big news story. "Tish. Are you there?" He tried to raise his girlfriend, but she couldn't hear him through her earpiece across the vast ballroom.

Tom pinched himself realizing if Crofton won, it would be a good money night. And if he could get Tish to figure out which end of the microphone to speak into, maybe he could snare some big-time interviews and make even more.

She was a good reporter, but she was only a few years out of college and worked for that newspaper down in DC. She was a print reporter. What did she know about broadcasting? Yet he had to give her credit, she stepped in at the last minute when he desperately needed her help. Now, if she could just master the equipment.

Tom had arrived early to set up his tripod and camera on the metal risers that stretched across the back of the room. At the time, there had been only one camera set up, of course in the best position, smack in the middle. So he'd taken the spot next to it. The platform was two feet above the ballroom floor to ensure all of the camera crews had a clear view of the stage.

CNN came out of an advertisement and a swelling orchestration of trumpets pervaded the room. Everyone looked up at the screen, watching a special golden election night logo glitter and spin into place.

"It's official," the bearded anchor resonated, "CNN projects Pennsylvania for Holly Crofton and that gives her enough electoral votes to become the first woman president of the United States."

The news reverberated into a rapturous eruption of jubilation throughout the ballroom. Tom tried to call Tish again. Nothing.

He opened a long zipper bag, pulled out his shotgun mike and attached it to the camera body and plugged in the power jack. He was glad he had invested in this specially modified mike. A pal, who was a sound engineer for a movie studio, had modified it for him to pick up sound from farther away than most shotguns and some of the smaller parabolics. It had covered his ass more than once in situations like this where he was restricted to the back of the room.

He made a couple of adjustments and looked for Tish again. He recognized the top of her head, those black curls were unmistakable in this crowd. She had her back to him, talking to someone. Then she turned in his direction. Now he would be able to pick up everything she said across the ballroom, even though she was a good hundred feet away.

She moved. He lost her. There. She was interviewing—what was his name? Crofton's press secretary, he thought.

He tapped his headset. Nothing. He had no sound feed. He zoomed in on Tish's face, adjusting his settings to her bronze skin.

"Tish? Tish?" She still couldn't hear him. What was going on? He pulled his headset off and sighed. The small jack attaching the headset cord wasn't fully seated.

This was his fault. He jammed it together, disgusted with himself, pulled the set over his head again and looked into his camera. Tish looked like she was only four feet away. And she looked damned good in that curve-hugging red jersey dress. He loved the optics of his video camera zoom lens—especially when it focused on Tish.

"Tish, can you hear me? Nod if you can hear me."

She did.

"Your mike is off." What a pair, he thought. Both of them were having trouble talking to each other. Funny, they never did as a couple. Alas, electronics had come between them.

He zoomed in on her hands.

"Flip the button on the bottom of the mike. The one under your right thumb."

He watched her manicured fingers. She did as she was told. She spoke into the mike.

"I still can't hear you. Got the second set of batteries?"

She nodded her head, unscrewed the bottom and dumped the rechargeable batteries into her hand while he watched it all through his camera lens. He let the camera run since it cost him nothing. God how he loved digital recording. He'd read stories in school about the old days when camera crews used their film sparingly because of its price and the additional cost of processing.

She pulled the extras from her pocket and loaded them.

"Can you hear me Tom?" she asked, speaking into the portable mike.

"Yep. We're back," he responded.

"Does this mean you missed my interview with Crofton's press secretary?"

"Afraid it does."

"Crap. He said some really good stuff."

Without saying a word, she turned back to the press secretary, who was now surrounded by a gaggle of reporters. Tish was three back in the pack behind some much taller male reporters and struggling to get closer. She extended her arm, shoving the mike between two reporters trying to pick up the secretary's comments.

Tom heard the commotion through his headset and adjusted the sound. He couldn't tell if he was picking it up from her microphone or the shotgun mike. No matter. He could edit and enhance it later.

He figured they were minutes away from Holly Crofton addressing her victory party and the boisterous crowd of supporters had gotten even louder and more compact. He felt the air conditioning kick in full blast from the ceiling vents high above. The ballroom was beginning to resemble a can of sardines. The air conditioning at least assured it wouldn't smell like one.

Tom didn't recognize most of the cameramen who set up next to him. He understood this was a national race, but usually the broadcast and cable networks sent the same local New York crews to Manhattan events.

He had been tempted once to join one of the networks. Several had wooed him, but he'd opted to remain an independent. He'd finally paid off his equipment and he liked the freedom of keeping his own hours and picking his own gigs.

For a moment he'd foolishly wondered if he'd made the right choice, especially when a documentary crew stole his regular freelance reporter at the last minute to cover Senator Berry's all-but-certain victory celebration across town at the Javits Center. The crew offered her nearly double his day rate. Maybe she'd think twice next time about abandoning him. He smiled. She was covering the loser and he had one of the best seats in town for one of the biggest presidential election upsets in United States history.

The place erupted. Tom looked up. Holly Crofton entered the stage from the left.

"She's here," he said, and turned his camera away from Tish toward the stage. He focused on the candidate—no, the president-elect—as she made her way through dozens of her staff and party dignitaries, hugging everyone within reach. This was her moment.

He glanced around the two-tiered platform. The camera next to him rested upon its tripod unmanned. He wondered if its owner got caught taking a smoke or was stuck in the men's room and couldn't make his way back through security. Maybe he lost his credentials. Tom thought for a split second of turning it on for him, doing a good deed, but then it moved.

He jumped back. It was operating on remote. He'd never seen a remote camera on a tripod covering a news event. He'd only seen them attached to a wall or ceiling as security cameras. But using one as a news camera? That was different. Where was the operator? In a satellite truck somewhere on the street? Must be a live feed. And Tom thought *he* was a small operator. At least he wasn't the only independent here tonight.

The crowd grew louder and he turned back to the task at hand.

President-Elect Crofton began to speak. "Thank you. Thank you." Her head bobbed in that now familiar motion. At one point during the campaign, he and a colleague joked about creating a Holly Crofton bobblehead doll. He had examined Holly's stagecraft and public performance and found it sorely lacking. As far as he was concerned, she had failed Campaigning 101. She couldn't give a speech. She came off as cold and uncaring. She was cardboard on stage.

And yet here she was.

What she lacked in campaign ability, well, she lacked in campaign ability. And her choice of a running mate wasn't much better. But last summer, after she'd added billionaire Derrick Templeton to the ticket as her vice-presidential choice, she jumped five points in the polls. Go figure. So much for Tom the political pundit. He would stick to his day job. He'd record the news and let the Croftons of the world make it.

He leaned over his camera and looked down, adjusting the view-finder to its proper angle so he wasn't craning his neck. He focused his camera close up on Crofton. As she began to thank her staff, he pulled back for his set shot, his lens taking in the entire stage and some of the true believers standing on the ballroom floor jockeying for position.

Templeton, a tall rotund bottle-blond with blotchy skin and a fake tan, was standing stage left with his third wife, a former model. At forty-five, she still had the trim figure, long legs and chiseled cheekbones of a sultry centerfold. Oh what money could buy, Tom thought.

He pulled his shot back more and panned the stage from left to right. Dozens of young staffers, family members and hangers-on were lucky enough to somehow make it on stage to witness history. Hugs abounded and dozens of disembodied arms were thrust aloft taking cell phone selfies or aimed at the crowd and Crofton, recording this special moment. History was a madhouse of joyous commotion.

Tom wondered if Tish could get anywhere near either Crofton or Templeton. Hell. She was the journalist. She'd know what to do—if she remembered how to switch on the microphone.

"Tish. Can you get to the other side of the stage?"

"I can't move," she said in his right ear. "Too many people."

"Damn. Let's hope they exit stage left. Maybe you can shove the mike in someone's face."

"I'll try."

He thought for a moment. Did Tish understand "stage left" was the right side of the stage—her side? Oh never mind. She'd figure it out if she got the opportunity.

He pulled back into an establishing shot and began to slowly zoom into a medium close-up of Crofton as she began her victory speech, rec-ognizing a long list of dignitaries and staff in the room. At least she got that part of politics right. The only people she didn't seem to thank were the hotel staff, probably because she didn't know every one of them by name. Tom smiled at the thought.

Then she began. "Tonight, the voters have spoken, and we love what they have had to say." Her voice was raw, just like the crowd. She was all bobblehead and stiff as a fence post, but it no longer mattered. The swarm of Secret Service agents surveying the crowd from in front of the stage attested to that.

"We are so grateful," she said, "to have the privilege to lead—"

A loud explosion rang out near Tom's left ear, and the concussion knocked him off his camera. He grabbed the side of his face, covered his ear, and looked toward the sound. Smoke and a small flame rose from the remote camera on the tripod next to him. It had exploded. He looked down. Pieces lay scattered on the platform carpet.

He instinctively reached for his camera to shield it from the fire, fearful the thing might explode again. That's when he heard the screams. They were muffled in his left ear, like he was underwater, but came through with startling clarity in his right headphone. He looked at the stage and saw Crofton collapsed in the arms of one of the men standing behind her. Her face and his were covered in blood.

What had happened? Was she stabbed? Shot?

Then he noticed everyone looking in his direction at the camera now smoldering on its tripod. Tom could smell the stench of plastic burning and another smell. What was it? Oh my God. Gunpowder. From the camera?

Instantly, two uniformed officers screamed at the videographers to move away from the blackened mass. Plastic parts were melting and dripping on the riser. Tom lifted his camera from its tripod and stepped back, away from the smoldering turmoil.

He slipped his camera on his shoulder and did what came naturally—recording the moment. He zoomed back and held his shot on the burning camera for several seconds and then turned to take in the bedlam infecting the ballroom. He swung his camera back to the stage. Several people huddled on their knees behind the podium. He couldn't see Crofton anywhere.

A dozen Secret Service agents appeared, guns drawn—serious guns drawn—blocking the stage. He saw more commotion on the stage to the left. It appeared like a shoving match. Then he saw a streak of platinum as the new vice president-elect was hustled off center stage—something his overwrought vanity would never do voluntarily.

Tom kept his camera rolling as he stepped down from the riser and into the ballroom mass. Screaming partisans everywhere were scrambling and supporters were falling and being trampled by friends as they pushed and shoved for the exits.

"Tom, Tom. Are you there?" Tish's voice frantically screamed through his headset.

"I'm here. You okay?"

"Yes. Where are you?"

"On the floor headed your way."

"I can't believe this. I can't see anything. They're saying Holly Crofton was shot."

"I'll make my way toward you. If you can find a door and can get out, do it. Or better yet, stand against the wall. You could get trampled. Keep talking to me. My camera is still on."

"I'm surrounded. I can't move. Too many people."

"Can you see anything?"

"A couple of Secret Service agents near me with guns, looking over the crowd. Some emergency medical techs on the stage," Tish said. "Now some Secret Service agents are circling the podium."

Tom swung his camera toward the stage, but he couldn't see anything. He turned back and pushed his way toward Tish.

"Please stay calm," a voice said over the public address system. Tom turned back again to see someone at the podium making a vain attempt to soothe the collective hysteria and retain a semblance of order. He tried to aim his camera as the true believers jostled and shoved him toward the exits, fending for themselves while many who had fallen lay helpless, screaming and curled in a protective fetal position on the ballroom floor.

He grabbed a small woman by the wrist. She had fallen to the floor. In one swift motion with his free arm, he hoisted her to her feet. She glanced at him, her face contorted in fear, and ran toward the exits.

Now he really feared Tish would get trampled in the free-for-all.

"I'm coming," he said into his headset. He elbowed his way forward.

"I'm not moving," Tish responded.

Finally, he made it to the corner by the stage and caught a glimpse of Tish's dark curls behind several people. He pushed his way between two tall men in dark suits and passed four women huddled together. He could hear sobs from behind him and screams through his good ear.

He set his camera on the floor between his legs and embraced her, keeping Tish safe from the tumult surrounding them.

Tom grabbed Tish's arm and his camera. He spied a closed door by the stage at the top of five steps. The masses were heading in the opposite direction. Their way was clear. He almost shoved her up the steps. She pushed on the door and it opened. He stepped through behind her. They were somewhere to the side of the stage.

Suddenly a swarm of people approached from their left. Tom pressed Tish against the wall, hoping not to get crushed. EMTs were running, wheeling Holly Crofton on a gurney. An IV was in her arm, her blouse was ripped open and an EMT was straddling her body riding on the gurney and pumping on her chest, performing CPR with both hands. Another EMT was racing beside the gurney pumping on a bag connected to a plastic tube that had been stuck down her throat.

A bloody towel had fallen away from her head revealing part of the back of her head was missing.

II

They followed the EMTs out the hotel to the sidewalk. Hundreds stood in shock, sobbing and dazed in disbelief. Tish watched the EMTs shove the stretcher into a waiting ambulance and it immediately pulled away from the curb with sirens screaming.

They were surrounded by confusion. She looked at him. Tom stood there, camera in hand, not taking pictures, Just staring, taking in the chaos.

"Tom," she said.

He didn't hear her.

"Tom." She grabbed his shoulder and their eyes met. "Tom, we need to get out of here." She knew his camera held valuable evidence. He needed to protect it and this was not the place.

"I'm going back in to see what I can learn," she said. "You head back to your apartment with your video before the police realize they want it. Make multiple copies just in case. I bet they'll come banging on your door looking for it."

He nodded, looking back at the hotel entrance. "My tripod is still in there."

"Really? At a time like this, you're worried about your tripod?"

"I just paid it off."

Her expression railed at him in disapproval. "I'll try to retrieve it if the cops will let me. Now go before they come looking for you."

He turned and seemed to take in the scene around him. Sirens blared in the distance, signaling more police were on their way. Several had already parked haphazardly across all traffic lanes, blocking anything from moving.

They looked at each other. The wailing crowd and the shrill sirens all became background noise as Tish struggled to absorb what they had both just witnessed. She smiled at him and instinctively brushed his cheek with the back of her hand, assuring their bond.

She felt a powdery substance between her fingers and looked at her hand. It was dark and gritty. "What's on your face?"

"Gunpowder, I think. From the explosion."

"Oh my God." She hadn't realized he might have been hurt in the explosion. "You're okay?"

"I'm fine."

"I didn't realize."

"I'm fine. Really."

This was no place to deal with this right now, she thought. "Okay. Take the subway. It's your only way out of this madhouse."

He nodded.

"I'll meet you back at the apartment as soon as I can."

They kissed and parted. She watched him walk briskly down the sidewalk with his camera in hand. She turned and headed back into the hotel.

Inside, the chaos continued. She looked for familiar faces and saw none. A policeman stood at the ballroom entrance stopping anyone from entering as dazed supporters continued to stagger out. She thought for a moment and headed back to the door leading to the stage where they had just exited. It was unguarded. She stepped into the back hallway where they had seen Holly Crofton bleeding from the head. How could she survive such a massive wound? Tish tried to put the thought out of her mind.

She slipped through the door that led back into the ballroom and silently walked down the steps. No one paid her any attention. Uniforms raced in every direction. There seemed to be no sense of order. Only confusion. The police were still clearing the crowd and securing the ballroom.

A group of uniforms and suits crowded over at the photographers' stand where Tom had set up. They were looking at what appeared to be a charred camera on a tripod. It was a black mess of melted plastic and metal. She grabbed her cell phone and discreetly took a video.

Tom had been standing next to that thing when it exploded. She closed her eyes thinking about it. He was okay. That's all that mattered.

Then she turned to the stage. Men and women in navy blue windbreakers with FBI in large white letters on the back placed plastic markers all over the floor, locating evidence. More likely pieces of Holly Crofton's brain, she thought. Tish could see blood and bits of red substance scattered on the floor. Her throat constricted. Oh God, not now, she told herself. She closed her eyes, willing her emotions. She couldn't afford to get sick. Not here.

Voices barking orders in the room finally revived her.

Tish looked up at the stage again, took several photos and quickly pocketed her phone and looked away, almost stumbling into three FBI agents. No political aides were left whom she could interview. Finally, she walked up to what appeared to be a city police detective and tried to ask him a question.

He glanced at her press ID hanging around her neck. "*Post-Examiner?* What are you doing here? Get out." He grabbed her by the forearm to escort her out of the ballroom. She pulled back.

"Take your hand off me," she demanded.

He did and gave her a stern look. "This is a crime scene. You must leave."

She did.

BACK IN THE LOBBY she saw a crowd of reporters hovered in the corner and then heard a familiar voice. It was Crofton's press secretary Lawrence Block. She ran over to listen. He was talking to someone on his telephone.

"Can you tell us her condition?" shouted a reporter.

"It's grave," the ashen-faced Block responded. He waved off questions and turned his back to the crowd. He put his finger in one ear and phone to the other.

The reporters kept screaming questions and he kept his back to them. It was apparent no one knew anything. She thought of the office. She needed to call.

Tish walked down a large hallway into the main lobby, far from the ballroom. Police were everywhere. She ducked into the bar at the end of the lobby and found an empty booth in the corner away from everyone. She emailed her photos to the City Desk just as a waiter walked up to take her order.

"Not now. I need a few minutes," Tish said and waved him off. "I need your table."

He backed away quietly. Word of Crofton's shooting had quickly spread throughout the building. She called the City Desk at the newspaper.

"I've just sent you photos of the crime scene from Holly Crofton's shooting," she told Meryl Maas, the deputy city editor. She heard computer keys clicking.

"I've got them. What else have you got?"

They were long past deadline for the final print edition of the newspaper. She knew the information she was relaying would appear on the newspaper's home page in a matter of minutes.

"She was shot. It appears one of the cameras or a cameraman in the back of the ballroom shot her. Not sure. The photo shows the suspicious video camera the FBI is looking at."

"A camera? She was shot with a camera?"

"All I can tell you is I heard an explosion and then she was shot. The camera—which was in the back of the ballroom on one of those stands where all of the photographers set up—exploded. I think some kind of hidden gun was inside it. When I saw Crofton being carried out by EMTs it appeared the back of her head was blown off, and her press secretary just reported her condition as grave."

"Great stuff," said Maas. "We'll add it to our main story. Have you seen Strobe Houghton? He sent us an initial report, but we haven't heard anything else yet."

"I haven't."

"Okay, keep feeding us stuff. By the way, why are you there? I thought you had the next few days off."

"I do. My boyfriend, who's a videographer, he was covering the party and needed my help."

"Well, we're damned lucky you're there. See what else you can find."

"Will do." If her information was important enough, she knew her desk editors would press to include it in whatever the national political reporters wrote about tonight. She might even get a credit at the end of the story.

Tish hung up. She headed for the subway. Thirty minutes later she reached Tom's apartment. He was already sitting at his computer editing his video.

"Find anything?" she asked before she had even closed and locked his front door.

"Look at this."

She dropped her bag on the couch and walked over to his kitchen table where he had set up his laptop. She looked at the screen.

He punched a key, and the video came on. Crofton was slurring her speech until Tish realized Tom was running the scene in slow motion. The impact of the bullet was immediate. Her head was flung back, blood spurted on several people directly behind her, and they all flinched instinctively. She collapsed into the arms of a man Tish did not recognize. The man held her for a moment, stunned, and then slowly lowered her to the floor.

"Can I send this to the paper?" she asked. "They'll pay, and I'll make sure you get a credit."

"Sure. Where to?"

She gave him Maas's email address and dictated a note he typed crediting him and signing it from Tish. The video of Crofton was gruesome. She decided to let her editors decide what readers could stomach.

Tom tapped on a few keys, and it was gone.

She called the desk.

"Got 'em?"

"Woo. I don't know if we can run this on the web page. That looks pretty bad."

"If nothing else, you know what you're dealing with," Tish said.

"You're right. We're looking at a President-Elect Templeton, or at least I think we are. We need to wake up our legal correspondents. I think we can stop hedging our bulletins about her condition. This will surely erase any tone of hope in our stories," Meryl said. "And to think just an hour ago she was on top of the world. We need to prepare our readers for the reality of what's about to happen. Oh God. This is so bad. I'll pass this on to the National Desk and let them decide what to publish."

Tish had never worked with the National Desk, which was why she called her bosses at the City Desk. They all knew her and took her seriously. The National Desk tended to be insular and arrogant, accepting only the word of their gray-haired reporters like Houghton.

"What will happen now?" Tish asked.

"I'm not sure," Meryl said. "I'll have to ask some of the national staff. They're the political pros. I guess this elevates Templeton. I don't know what else could happen."

"Wasn't he, well, some kind of a bombastic fool on the campaign trail? Is that an act or the real thing?" Tish asked.

"From what I hear around the office, it's all real. But I've got to think a lot of it was just campaign bluster. Looks like we'll find out soon enough."

"Yeah," Tish hung up and turned to Tom, who was still feverishly hammering away at his laptop, editing video. She peered over his shoulder for a minute. He was editing some footage she had already seen.

"I'm going to change," she said.

He barely acknowledged her.

She walked into his bedroom and stripped, tossing her dirty blouse and underwear in Tom's hamper and hanging up her dress in his tiny closet. She found a T-shirt in the drawer and slipped it on. It was his Yankees baseball T-shirt. She liked it for its comfort and that it fell to mid-thigh. It was the most comfortable piece of clothing in his apartment to lounge in.

She walked back in the living room and turned on the television to one of the all-news channels. They had called in a law professor to talk about the sticky constitutional question should Crofton not survive. She flipped to another network where some of the gruesome footage was playing. Tom heard it and rose from the table and walked closer to watch.

It was a wide shot showing happy supporters on the ballroom floor and Crofton standing at the podium. Then pandemonium broke loose. From her spot over in the corner of the room near the stage, Tish had not realized the extent of the panic that had ensued. She saw people run for the exits, screaming. Some stood, staring at the stage in shock at what they had just witnessed. The camera wide shot was far enough back that it did not show the gruesome details included in Tom's video footage.

"I recognize that guy," he said, talking about the camera work. "He shoots good stuff. He was down at the far end of the riser."

"Would you show me the rest of yours?" Tish asked.

She turned the volume down on the television and stepped to the table, pulling up a chair beside Tom's.

It started out with video of her interviewing Crofton's press secretary with no sound. He showed a close-up of her changing the batteries in her microphone and hurrying back to the press huddle. And then the money shots of the shooting and the loud bang. His camera had shaken and gone haywire for a moment.

"I was thrown off here by the explosion," he said.

"Really?"

"The camera next to mine was run by remote. Now I understand why. Here. Listen."

He backed up the footage to moments before the shooting. "Hear that whirring sound?"

She could barely make it out.

"It's the sound of the camera swiveling and the lens adjusting—at least that's what I think it is. Can you hear it?"

Even with the din of the crowd, yes, she could hear it—the sound of the camera moving.

"The remote device had to be a modified camera of some sort," said Tom. "Or at least a gun designed to look like a camera. But it had to have a camera inside to help it aim. Imagine that. Probably had a zoom lens with crosshairs. Whoever was running it had all day to focus in on Crofton. She wasn't fifty yards away. It would be like ducks in a barrel."

"You mean like shooting fish in a barrel," said Tish.

"Whatever."

"But why did it burn up?"

"I gotta think because it was so small, and it had to house both the gun and camera and still look like a real camera, it couldn't handle the heat of the explosion of firing the bullet. I'll bet it was designed for only one shot. I'm surprised it didn't fall backward off the riser from the kickback of the shot. Instead, it just stood there and smoldered. Here, look at this."

He rolled the footage forward again, through the shooting, through the initial impact of the shot. They watched his video of the destroyed camera. A small flame was coming out of the side and smoke was rising.

"Wait. Look here," Tom said pointing to the screen. "There's a small sandbag at the bottom holding the tripod in place. Who does that?"

"Oh my God. We need to get this out there. Can I send it to my newspaper?"

"Sure."

"Okay. But I'm sending it to my clients too. I've already got a dozen messages from all over the country and three from overseas. They all want my video feed. It's going to be a long night."

Tish looked at the clock. It was two in the morning. She had forgotten how long it had taken for the final state tallies to come in giving Crofton the win. It had been almost midnight when she had approached the podium.

Tom emailed the video of the damaged camera and Tish got back on her phone to the City Desk.

"Amazing. This is great stuff," said Meryl. "We're going to be first out of the gate with it. And sound and video just after it happened. Great work, Tish."

"Thank Tom. It's his work."

"But you're on top of it and getting it to us so quickly. I wish Houghton was so responsive," she said.

"What happened to him?"

"He's at the hospital twiddling his thumbs along with ten thousand other reporters awaiting word from the doctors. He's phoned in a couple of times with nothing new to add. Your material is the only thing new we've added to our stories. Thanks to your reporting we're ahead of the pack. No one has our exclusives, and the cable networks are starting to credit us with some of their coverage. They're even buying some of the rights to your photos and footage, so tell your boyfriend to work up an invoice quickly. We're going to owe him a lot of money."

"He'll be happy to hear that," Tish said. She hung up and smiled to herself. She was proud of Tom. Proud that he was better than those goons who usually carried their cameras traipsing around with some network correspondent. He had real ambition. Not only did he create great video, but he had an artistic side. He had been an art major before switching to photography in college, and it showed.

She turned to Tom. "Meryl just told me we've gone viral. Some of my pictures and some of your video they posted online got picked up by the networks."

She walked over to the television and turned up the volume again. She sat on the couch with the remote and began flipping channels. She wanted to see for herself what the all-news networks were reporting.

A male network anchor chimed in: "This just in. The Washington *Post-Examiner* reports the shot that gravely injured President-Elect Holly Crofton apparently came from a remote device disguised as a video camera. It was set up in the back of the ballroom aside dozens of photographers who were on a riser videoing the event. We have not yet confirmed this with authorities, who are still declining to comment on this evening's shooting."

"Tom," she called. "We're leading the news."

He hustled to the television to listen to the anchor repeat what he had just reported and ask other reporters seated around a glass table on the set for their take.

"Oh my God. I can't believe it," Tom said.

They watched more as his video of the burning camera was aired. When they finally went to a commercial, she looked at Tom and smiled.

"I've got one more thing to show you," he said.

She forgot they hadn't finished watching his video. They quickly sat at the kitchen table again in front of Tom's computer as he fingered a few keys. The video jostled as he moved across the room toward Tish. She could tell he had placed it on the floor when they had found each other and hugged. And then it moved up the steps, thigh high, as he carried it to the back hallway. And then, oh God, it was right at the level where Crofton was wheeled out of the building, still running. Crofton's condition was more gruesome than Tish had remembered.

"I need to get this to my bosses."

"You sure? No one will run this."

"I know. But they can describe what they saw."

"I don't know."

"Tom, trust me. People need to know what we saw. They don't need to see it for themselves."

They sat together as he emailed the last of his video footage to Tish's City Desk editors.

Tish was on the phone.

"Got it again. Tish, you are really outdoing the competition tonight. You're making them all look like fools speculating about everything while we're repeatedly providing the facts. And Houghton, jeez, that old fossil is sitting on his ass all night giving us nothing. Girl, you've done the City Desk proud. Great work."

Tish hung up. For the first time all night, she felt a bit of elation. She loved the buzz of working on a big story, but this one was so tragic. Her feelings were all mixed up.

She sat on the couch again and felt the weight of the late hour, but her adrenaline blocked any thought of sleep. She watched the news for another hour as Tom worked his computer editing video and sending it to clients. She laid her head on a couch pillow and caught every third word the television news anchor was saying as her eyelids struggled with consciousness.

"Crofton...shot...Templeton...ballroom...electoral win...upset... grave..."

III

When Tish awoke, sun was streaming through the blinds. She pulled herself up, recognizing she was still on Tom's couch in the living room. Sometime during the night, Tom had taken the old ratty blanket on the back of his couch and covered her with it. She turned and saw Tom still at his computer, still sitting at the kitchen table.

"Honey, are you ever going to bed?"

"Twenty-seven requests for footage, babe. Gotta strike while the iron is hot. I'm going to make more than seventeen thousand dollars from this. Maybe even twenty. I haven't begun to add up the invoices."

The television was still running, but Tom had muted the volume. She stood, picked up the remote from the coffee table, and turned the sound up.

Political pundits were still discussing Tom's video, but with an ominous tone. They had picked up the verbiage from the *Post-Examiner* website, which described an eyewitness account of Crofton's condition, saying much of the back of her skull was missing.

She realized that except for the network's own video, she and Tom were the source for most of the breaking news. Where were the other reporters? Had they learned nothing overnight? Had the government buttoned it down so tightly, that quickly?

Then the anchors started another conversation about what might happen next, and the discussion turned to Templeton.

"They don't want to state the obvious," said Tom.

"Which is?"

"They've been dancing around Crofton's condition all night. It's only a matter of time, but they are being polite. It's bad taste, I suspect, to talk about President-Elect Templeton."

Tish hadn't considered that. Templeton would likely become the president-elect and, come January 20, the next president of the United States. She knew little about him, but what she'd heard wasn't flattering.

Then a big banner saying "Bulletin" flashed across the screen.

"CNN has confirmed that President-Elect Holly Crofton has died. Repeat. She died from wounds suffered early this morning, when an assassin shot her as she was giving her victory speech. Repeat, Holly Crofton, the upset victor in yesterday's presidential election, has died."

Tish turned down the volume. She glanced at Tom who had looked up from his laptop and was glued to the television from across the room.

"Unbelievable," he said.

"I can't wrap my head around it," said Tish. "And we were eyewitnesses."

She looked at Tom. He looked awful after being up all night.

"Don't you think you should get some sleep?"

"Yeah. I should get a few hours I guess." He tapped on his laptop keys again, then paused and closed the lid. "Don't let me sleep too long. I moved all the video but one, and I still have a lot of invoicing to do."

He stood from the kitchen table and walked back to the bedroom. Tish realized he hadn't even taken off his shoes since last night. The bedroom door closed, and she heard the shower running in the bathroom. She turned back to the television. They were discussing Crofton's political career. Her cell phone rang.

"Tish, you heard?" asked Meryl.

"Just saw it."

"The campaign just put out a notice that Templeton will make a statement at eleven. I want you there."

"What about Houghton?"

"Listen, if we want to rely on press releases, we can rely on Houghton. The City Desk swamped National last night because of your work. You may not get a byline so the public knows who's doing the work, but the newsroom sure knows. Now do the City Desk proud."

"Well, sure. I guess so."

"I'll text you the details. Remember. Eleven o'clock." Meryl hung up.

Nobody in the news business was getting any sleep, thought Tish.

Except for last night, she had never covered anything to do with presidential candidates or political campaigns. Heck, she'd been with the *Post-Examiner* for what—ten months? She was still covering local city council and board of supervisors meetings. Now she'd have to go act like she knew what she was doing on the national stage. Better to just try not to embarrass herself.

She listened for the shower to stop. When it was done, she stepped into Tom's bedroom. He was already in bed with the blinds closed. She pulled her T-shirt over her head and dropped it at the foot of the bed and tiptoed into the bathroom, which connected to the bedroom. It was something she didn't like about his small apartment, but then in New York, you settled for what you could get.

She closed the door behind her as she entered the steamy room. She turned on the hot water. It was heavenly.

A half hour later she was eating breakfast, downing a cup of coffee, and checking her text messages for details about the press conference. It was halfway across town. She checked her watch. A quarter to ten. She needed to get moving. She left Tom a note next to his computer, packed her laptop in her shoulder bag, and headed out the door.

She arrived about fifteen minutes early and went through a metal detector and bag search to enter another hotel ballroom. A man in a dark suit scrutinized her press pass in great detail. The Secret Service appeared to be putting on a display of extra security given last night's catastrophe. A little late now for that, she thought.

Tish didn't know much about the Constitution and succession except what she'd learned in high school, but the television commentators had said last night that should Crofton not survive, Templeton was all but certain to become the next president. It was up to the Electoral

College now, but what choice did they have? A bunch of Democratic Party electors weren't likely to vote for a Republican.

The hotel was across from Templeton Tower where the future president lived on the top floor with his ex-model wife—a gorgeous woman from Russia. Tish had read about her in *Vanity Fair*, which had published nude photos of her from her modeling career. How weird. Anyone now could see the future First Lady in all her glory on the internet. That was a first.

The room was packed with probably two hundred reporters. She'd never seen anything like this. She still struggled to absorb the events of the last twelve hours. She suspected others in the room were doing the same—operating on an adrenalin high, keeping one foot in front of the other. After all, she knew this was what many of them lived for.

She recognized a couple of television correspondents and a pundit from the *New York Times*. Otherwise, she knew no one in the room. She hadn't even met Houghton, the *Post-Examiner's* national political reporter who had covered Crofton's campaign. She wondered if he had even heard of her or knew she was now his backup.

A commotion set off from the left. Tish watched a stream of Secret Service agents enter and scatter across the room. A podium stood at center stage. Agents stood on either side and in front on the ballroom floor. She noticed several in the back of the room monitoring all the photographers and videographers.

Tish was about five rows back. She pulled out her notebook and jotted down a description of the room and the crowd of journalists. The first was modern, bright and shiny. The second was wrinkled, weary and badly in need of a shower.

Another commotion. This time it was Templeton walking on stage. He went straight for the podium and grabbed both sides as if he were going to give it a hug. Tish wondered if he would be unsettled before a worldwide audience focused entirely on him for the first time.

He adjusted his gaze, apparently searching for the words on a teleprompter. He squinted and shielded his face with his hand, trying to see his audience beyond the klieg lights.

"It's with great sadness that I stand before you today," he read. "I want to personally offer my condolences to Holly Crofton's entire family. Today, the nation mourns with you."

So far, so good, she thought.

"After I finish my remarks, Professor Frederick Franklin of the Yale University Law School will discuss the Constitutional ramifications of what has just taken place. But today is a day of mourning for all Americans. I'll now ask Monsignor Eugene LeCouter to offer a prayer."

Templeton conceded the podium to a Catholic priest, who bowed his head. Tish was not a believer and watched in silence as everyone on stage stared at the floor. She wondered how many on stage were truly religious instead of just standing there pretending to be reverent. She paid little attention to the priest's words. They meant nothing to her. She had left the church nearly a decade ago, during her freshman year of high school, after a priest she had admired nearly raped her. Only a quick knee to his groin had saved her dignity and virginity.

When the monsignor was done, Templeton wrestled with the podium again as if he were holding the love of his life in his arms. And maybe he was. He stood there a moment saying nothing. Then the reporters erupted with questions.

He waved his right hand. "No questions. This is not the proper time or place. We're all in mourning today. Let's take a moment. It's a very important moment. One of the most important moments in our nation's history. It's sad. So very, very sad."

Going off script? She held her phone in the air to assure the app recorded every word.

"We are the greatest country on Earth. Whoever did this will be brought to justice," he said. "I will not rest until I find Holly Crofton's killer. She was a good woman. A fine woman. A great woman. A great running mate. We were a great team, Holly and me. We were great friends. I will get to the bottom of this, and when I do, they will pay dearly."

More shouts from the reporters. He looked around and then turned back and looked at his people behind him as if asking what to do next. He then grabbed the podium again.

"It's now up to me to lead this great nation. Lyndon Johnson was the last president to face a situation like this. He was a great president. He rose to the occasion. So will I. You will see over the next four years. I will be a great leader for America."

He sounded like he was delivering a campaign speech somewhere in middle America.

"This country will be great again. No assassin is going to bring us down," he said. "God bless America."

He turned his back on the crowd and greeted some of the people standing behind him. Then he turned and waved at the reporters, all of whom were yelling questions in his direction.

Tish got up from her seat and headed for the door. She knew his penthouse was in his own high-rise across the street. Perhaps she could get closer outside on the sidewalk.

She stepped onto the concrete and smelled car exhaust in the cool morning air. She stepped around the side of the building onto Fifth Avenue and saw a door surrounded by police officers. She waited with a crowd of onlookers. Then he appeared. He was wearing a long, black overcoat and looked unusually fat this morning. Then she realized the Secret Service probably forced him to wear a bulletproof vest under his coat just to walk across the street. He began shaking hands with the crowd as the agents anxiously watched. Agents were on either side of him, their arms raised, ready to swat away any harmful gestures from the public.

When Templeton reached her in the crowd, he grabbed her hand and Tish reacted on instinct.

"Mr. Templeton, how do you feel about last night?"

He paused and looked her in the eye. "Terrible tragedy. But I will be the best president this country has ever seen. The best. I will make this country great again. Holly Crofton could never have done that."

He looked at her and tilted his head as his eyes traveled down her chest and back to her eyes again. "Nice," he said. "You're a hot little number."

Then he moved down the line of bystanders shaking more hands as the Secret Service nudged him along.

Tish felt her cheeks blush. If she weren't biracial, she thought, someone in the small crowd might see her blush in anger. The future president of the United States had just sized her up and described her as a hot little number. Was she supposed to feel flattered? The next president of the United States had just visually groped her. It was as if he were examining a piece of meat hanging on a hook. And in front of all of these people.

She turned to a short, middle-aged, overweight woman next to her. "Did you hear what he just said to me?" she asked.

"I sure did, honey. Lucky you, dear. The president thinks you're cute," the woman said. "Did you see him touch me? He actually shook my hand. I touched the next president of the United States." She put her hands to her face and rocked back on her heels.

Maybe she was just overreacting, Tish thought. Fortunately, she could let her editors decide. She tapped her phone and sent the entire Templeton recording to Meryl.

A whiff of salt and warm bread tempted her nostrils. A street vendor was hawking soft pretzels at the corner. She stopped, purchased one and decided to walk awhile to burn off the calories. She could use time to clear her head.

Tish wasn't scheduled to be back at work until tomorrow, yet she'd been working ever since she'd arrived in New York. She hoped she got some credit for everything she'd done. She'd put it on her timesheet when she returned. She needed the money. Maybe she could even get some overtime. Being at the bottom of the union pay scale at the newspaper was, well, tough. And she'd just moved out of a group house and rented a new apartment in DC. At least she could bum off her boyfriend for a place to stay here in New York.

Her phone rang.

"How did you get that?"

It was Meryl again.

"Don't you ever sleep?" Tish asked.

"This is the biggest story of my career. I'll sleep when the caffeine runs out. Now where did you get that audio?"

"I caught him outside the hotel after his speech as he was walking back to his condo."

"Tish, you just keep those headlines coming. You realize we have the future president making a pass at you and trashing his running mate less than ten hours after she died? Who does that?"

"Apparently, you now know."

"Great work. You keep making the City Desk and yours truly look good. We haven't even heard from Houghton yet, and we're about to put your audio on the web. Keep it up."

Tish hung up and kept walking. The world had gone mad and she was thrust right in the middle of a global insane asylum. The speed and the breadth at which news traveled was astounding. Templeton says something outrageous and minutes later the whole world knows about it. And here she was, walking down a sidewalk in the middle of New York City and no one even recognizes her, yet she just talked to millions around the world.

She had just played a small role in history. The idea made her light-headed. And to think less than a year ago, she had been working at a small town daily writing about city council. Her twenty-fifth birthday was only a few months off. Where would she be by then?

IV

He stared at the ceiling, languishing in the luxury of his bed. Tom glanced down to see Tish sitting at the foot; her gleaming brown eyes and wide smile greeted him with warmth. She had such an attractive face, her smooth light brown expression contoured by exotic ringlets.

He lifted himself on his elbows, savoring the moment. She was wearing a tight blue sweater, which accentuated her small, firm breasts. They seemed larger because she was so slender. He appreciated that she worked out to keep her figure. It was a good thing, because she loved to eat rich food when they went out to dinner. She never much cared about counting calories.

She edged up the bed and bent over and kissed him. He rolled her over onto the bed and held her tight, their kiss never interrupted. He ran his hand through her curls and then caressed her right breast. He realized she was wearing a bra.

"You're dressed?" he said, their faces only inches apart.

"It's afternoon. I've been to a press conference with Templeton already."

"Oh Jesus." He jumped out of bed.

"What?"

"I've still got to send footage to a station in Japan. I'm late." He ran into the kitchen and flipped open his laptop. Tish followed him. Several keystrokes later, the video was gone.

"Their tech wasn't due in until noon our time." He looked at the clock on the wall. It was shortly after one.

"Let's catch our breath," said Tish. "I want to talk about the last twenty-four hours."

She made a pot of coffee and toasted some bagels and walked into the living room. Tom finally pulled on a pair of pajama bottoms and T-shirt and joined her on the couch. They talked about last night and how their work influenced last night's news coverage. Then they got to the gruesome scene they had witnessed.

"Should we talk to someone? A counselor? That was pretty gruesome, seeing her on the stretcher like that," Tish said.

Tom remembered the scene and then his video, which was too explicit for any network to air. "Let it sit for a few days. If it's still really bothering you, I'm happy to go with you."

Tish stood and walked around to the back of the couch, leaned over and hugged him around the neck from behind. "You are the sweetest man."

Just then they heard a knock on Tom's front door. "Who could that be?" Tom walked to the door and looked through the peephole. He turned to Tish and whispered, "It looks like the feds."

"Quick. Hide your computer," she said. "Did you make a copy?"

He handed her a thumb drive.

Another knock sounded at Tom's front door. "FBI," came a muffled voice from the other side.

Tom opened the door. Two men in suits stood there. One flashed a badge.

"Tom O'Neal?"

"Yes."

"You were one of the photographers at the Crofton victory party last night?"

"Yes."

"We'd like to talk to you about your video from last night. We need a copy."

Tom turned to Tish. "What do you want it for?" she asked. Tish stepped from behind Tom to face the agents.

"Part of our investigation into the assassination of Holly Crofton. We're collecting video from all of the photographers who were at the event. It's just routine."

Tom looked at her. This was the moment she had told him to expect. The reason he had made copies. They looked at each other and she nodded.

"We were expecting you, but maybe not so soon," said Tish. "Do you have a warrant?"

"As you might imagine, we've been very busy all night. The future president was murdered. If you need a warrant, we will come back with one. We ask that you not destroy your video. This is a matter of national security."

Tish looked at Tom. He raised an eyebrow silently saying, "What the hell?"

She turned to the agents and held out the thumb drive. "Here. This is a copy of everything."

"We appreciate your cooperation," the agent said. "We're all in this together." The agent thanked them again and then he and his colleague turned and walked down the hall.

Tom locked the door and sat at the kitchen table. Tish took his hand and led him back into the living room. "Let's sit in comfort," she said. They renewed their conversation as if the feds had never shown up. Tish reminded him she needed to return to Washington tomorrow.

"It seems I didn't get a day off like I had hoped."

They both laughed.

"Let's do something fun this afternoon. I can send invoices tomorrow," Tom said.

Just then they heard another knock on Tom's front door. This time Tish rose and checked the peephole.

"Tom?" She turned to him.

He realized something was wrong by her tone and approached the door. He looked through the peephole. Two more suits. This time a man and a woman.

He opened it a crack, leaving the chain on the door.

"FBI," said the woman, and flashed her badge. "Tom O'Neal?"

"Stop," Tom said. "What the hell is going on?"

The agents looked puzzled.

"Aren't you one of the videographers filming last night's Crofton victory party?"

"I was. But your guys have already been here."

"What?"

"Yeah. They asked for a copy of my video and just left a few minutes ago."

"That wasn't the FBI," said the woman in the dark suit.

"What do you mean?"

"I mean we're the agents assigned to find all of the video taken of the assassination. No other agents are handling this part of the investigation."

Tom looked at Tish. Her mouth hung open, and her eyes widened. What was going on?

V

"We need to see more ID than just your badge," Tish demanded.

Both agents pulled out their business cards, slipping their contact information through the barely opened door. She read them. Special Agents Kathy Mueller and Jake McCabe.

"How do I know any of this is real?" she asked.

"Call the number. It's the main number for the New York office," Mueller said.

Tish looked up the New York office of the FBI online. The numbers matched. She made the call. After talking with several people, she affirmed their identity.

Finally, she felt comfortable enough to invite them in. Tom unlatched the chain on the door, and Tish motioned the agents to the couch. Their patience, she could tell, had been tested.

Tom began to tell their story. The agents listened intently, taking notes.

"Can you describe these two individuals?" asked McCabe.

They painted an image of two broad-shouldered men with round eyes and short-cropped hair. Tish realized it wasn't much to go on. Frankly, she told them, she might have trouble recognizing them if they walked in the room right now. Tom, ever the photographer, said he'd have no trouble picking them out of a lineup.

They huddled around Tom's laptop, watching the video. Tom frequently stopped to explain what was happening around them at the time. The agents scribbled madly on their notepads. This went on for two hours.

Finally, Tom gave them a thumb drive with a second copy of his unedited video, but not until Mueller handed him a warrant. The agents had come prepared and even gave Tom a receipt acknowledging they had received the copy.

Tish realized how naïve they had been. Had she and Tom only known what to expect when the first set of so-called agents arrived, they'd have handled it differently.

As soon as Tom showed the agents to the door and closed it behind them, he turned to her. "What did those other guys want with my video? This makes no sense."

Tish looked at him. "I agree. Most of what you took has already been broadcast, on the web, or written about. What do they think they will find?"

"That's it," Tom said. "They're looking for something that took place in that ballroom and wondering if I captured it on video. Something that hasn't been broadcast. They found out it was my video everyone was broadcasting."

"And you thought none of the television networks gave you credit last night for your work," Tish said. She poked him playfully in the shoulder.

"I guess they did," Tom said.

They looked at each other for a moment. It was like they were thinking the same thing. Tom tilted his head toward the kitchen table and Tish nodded. He picked up his laptop from the coffee table where they had been watching it with the agents and walked it over to the old linoleum kitchen table again. He plugged in the power cord and they sat down side by side and began to watch from the beginning.

It took nearly thirty minutes to run through the entire recording. They did it in real time, not stopping once.

Nothing.

"We don't know what we are looking for," Tish said. "If we just had a clue."

"Or maybe I was not in the right position to record whatever they're looking for."

"Let's look for those two fake agents. Maybe they're in the crowd."

They didn't have to wait long. Near the beginning of the video, when Tom had been trying to explain to Tish how to change the batteries in her microphone, he froze on a shot of the crowd behind her. They zoomed in, moving from face to face. Then, not ten feet from Tish, they recognized one of the men. Tom zoomed in until the picture pixilated—too grainy to make out. He zoomed back a little and pressed print. They continued to look, and about five feet from the first fake FBI agent was the second. He looked full-faced into Tom's camera, as if he were watching Tom video him from across the room.

"Maybe that's why they came for the video," Tom said. He printed a copy of the second man. "We should give these to the FBI."

"You've got their card. Email it to them," Tish said.

As he was emailing the stills, Tish's cell phone rang. "It's Meryl. Can you stay in New York for a while? We'd like you to cover Templeton and the assassination investigation for the next several days."

"I guess so, but what about Houghton?"

"Don't care," said Meryl. "You've been leading the pack on this story with exclusives. Stay there. Keep reporting."

Tish looked around the apartment. Tom certainly wouldn't mind. Then she remembered she'd packed for only two days. "I haven't anything to wear. I was scheduled to come back tomorrow."

"No worries. Buy a couple of outfits. I'll take it out of petty cash. Can you stay with your boyfriend rather than in a hotel?"

"Of course."

"Good. I can justify you expensing your clothes. That's a lot cheaper than paying for a hotel."

"How do you know that?"

"I know your taste in clothes."

That stung. Tish hadn't thought about her office attire not being up to standard. Since she arrived at the newspaper no one had ever said anything about her appearance. But she was guilty of not being a fashion maven. She always thought she was being practical. She had several suits and skirts and always looked professional. Maybe it was time she paid more attention to her appearance. Although on her salary, she couldn't afford the expensive attire she noticed on the more senior women in the newsroom.

"If I'm going to cover Templeton, I need to get my butt in gear and get to the store immediately. Any retailer you prefer?"

"Nordstrom or Bergdorf's will do," Meryl said. "Represent us well. And just a few outfits. National will send reinforcements there soon. Houghton has a thumb sucker to finish for the Sunday edition and then he is off on vacation. He never suspected he'd actually be covering the winner. National's agreed to use you in the interim as back up. Of course, you and I know that's bullshit. The City Desk has been knocking the crap out of National on the story since it began. In my book you don't back up anybody. Now go kick some ass."

"Thanks." Tish clicked off her cell. Tom was fiddling with his laptop. She needed to get moving. But where did she begin covering Templeton? She just heard her boss's disdain for sitting around waiting for press statements. That wasn't in her DNA anyway.

She grabbed her purse and dug through it looking for Jim Grant's business card. Crofton's Press Secretary Lawrence Block had given her his deputy's contact information last night while they were talking and told her to call Grant, not him, if she needed anything. It was his way of politely blowing her off as he cut short her interview to talk to some network correspondents. She dialed, and Grant picked up on the third ring.

"It's Tish Woodward with the *Post-Examiner*. I met Lawrence Block last night, and he gave me your number. I'm so sorry about everything that has happened. You and the entire campaign staff must be devastated."

"Thanks. It's been a rough time for sure," said Grant.

"I've been assigned on a temporary basis to cover Derrick Templeton. Since I don't know anyone on the campaign, I was hoping we could have a background conversation."

He said nothing. She felt uncomfortable waiting for him to speak. Finally...

"After what I observed last night, I was almost thinking of calling you," Grant said. "That was your stuff all over the *Post-Examiner*, on the internet, and on cable. You broke most of the story. Not bad for someone who wasn't even covering the campaign. I'm impressed. Sure, I'll meet with you, but let's keep this on the Q-T. You know Patrick McManus near Wall Street?"

"No, but I'll find it."

"It's an Irish pub."

"I figured."

"Let's make it three thirty. We'll have the place to ourselves." He gave her the address.

"Thanks."

She hung up. She'd talk to him first and then go clothes shopping.

VI

Grant was right. When she walked in the door, the bar was empty. It was also old and beat up, like a thoroughbred racehorse past its prime and no longer collecting stud fees. It was out to pasture with nothing to do but take up space and time. It got that privilege because of what it once was, she guessed.

Grant sat in the far corner with his back to the wall, a beer in front of him and a plate of pickles with mustard on the side. He was dabbing his pickles with his long fingers into the mustard and crunching away.

He stood when she approached the table, wiping his fingers with a cloth napkin. They shook hands. She reluctantly. He motioned her to sit.

"You have no idea how much I appreciate this," she said. "Like I told you, I've been temporarily assigned to back up Strobe Houghton covering the Templeton transition. My newspaper is sending reinforcements to cover him but wants me to help with the transition. Houghton—I assume you know Strobe—is doing a big piece for the Sunday paper and then sails off on a long-planned vacation with his wife. He never figured Crofton to win."

"Neither did we," Grant said. He shook his head of thick, reddish-brown hair and smiled. His unshaven face was drawn. Tish could tell he had had little rest since last night.

"We're so unprepared for any transition it's not even funny. We all thought we'd get drunk last night, clean out our desks today, and take a cue from Houghton and stick our bare feet in the sand somewhere far away from here."

Tish grabbed her reporter's notepad.

"Before I go any further," Grant said, "this is all on background as you said over the phone. Nothing on the record. My name shows up nowhere. Agreed?"

"Absolutely. I just need to get my bearings."

"I'm impressed with your reporting so far. And I don't even know you. I did a quick background on you. What are you? Twenty-five?"

"Twenty-four."

"And you've done a lot of investigative reporting. All local stuff—but pretty good. I pulled up some of your stories. Why aren't you on the National Desk?"

"I'm twenty-four."

Grant smiled. "Got it. Looks to me like you'll certainly earn your spurs on this one if they give you a chance."

"Don't forget. Female."

"Ah yes, the old sexist newsroom culture. Lived that before."

"Not everyone in the newsroom," she said. "But enough."

"Then how did you get assigned to Templeton?"

"Complete accident. I had last night off, so I was helping my boyfriend. He was one of the cameramen in the back at last night's victory party. In fact, he was standing right next to that camera-gun-thingy that exploded, which appears to be what killed Crofton."

Then she remembered her manners. "Jim, I'm sorry about Crofton. Were you guys close?"

"As close as anyone, which means not close at all. But we were loyal to each other. It was like when I played football in high school. We were a tight-knit group."

"I hope you're doing okay."

"It was a team not a marriage. I guess right now we're all in shock. I mean, our entire nation's history turned on a dime last night. Just like that." He snapped his fingers. "Last night is so difficult to fathom. I wouldn't say it's a real personal loss for me. Don't get me wrong. She was a friend, but she was also a pain in the ass."

He looked straight ahead and not at her and then took a long gulp of his beer and grabbed another pickle.

"Care for one?"

"One?"

"Pickle." He wagged it over the plate. "Quite good here."

"Uh. No thanks." She suddenly was aware she was wrinkling her nose.

He chomped down again, apparently not noticing. "Your reporting is pretty damned impressive," he said with a full mouth of pickle. "Here's the thing. There are no investigative reporters covering Templeton. Never were. Plenty there to look into. I mean he was just another pretty face on the campaign trail. No one really cared. They never do about the number two on the ticket—especially if he is going to lose."

He smiled, waving another pickle for emphasis.

"It was all about his money, wasn't it?" Tish asked.

"You bet your ass. He opened the floodgates of Wall Street for us. So much money flooded into the campaign, not even those rich asshole Republicans could keep up with us. The campaign was really smoking at the end there. We kept creeping up, yet no one on staff thought we had a chance in hell to win. But the Wall Street money really gave us a boost. Otherwise, Templeton's contributions were nil.

"He's nothing more than a bigmouthed oaf. Undisciplined, unread, poorly educated. But hey, he attracted those same voters to our cause. He gave us our two-point margin of victory last night. I gotta give him credit for that. We would not have won without him. I'm told he has a charming side. I just haven't experienced it yet."

"How much did your campaign work with his?" Tish asked.

"At first we thought the two candidates would be a team, but it became clear after a few weeks, he did his own thing. We did get him to agree not to speak ill of Crofton. Believe me, they were not friends. This was a business arrangement. Crofton was used to that. Her marriage was a sham. She was sleeping with her campaign manager."

"You're kidding."

"That's off the record," he said. He took another swig of beer and a waiter came by. Tish ordered a club soda. "Almost every night. Almost every hotel on the road. No one ever questioned why the campaign manager spent so much time on the trail with the candidate. I mean, from a tactical point of view, it made no sense. Word was she couldn't get enough of him. I guess the woman was sex-starved in her own marriage. Or maybe she just needed some affection from someone. Everybody knows you don't get it on the campaign trail—except from the crowds. Everyone else is pulling you in a different direction. They all want a piece of your time. It's not a fun place to be."

He took another gulp from his mug. "I don't really care about her sex life. She was going to make one hell of a president. Imagine Crofton as the first female president of the United States."

He looked at Tish through the lens of the bottom of his beer glass and signaled the waiter for another. "You really are a virgin in this territory, aren't you?"

Tish felt insignificant for a moment. "I've covered a lot of local politics, but nothing on the national scene. Last night was my first time and it was never intended that I do anything much more than stand in for my boyfriend's hired help. Tom is an independent videographer and his freelance reporter got a better gig at the last minute."

"Lucky for you. You've got instincts. And as I was saying earlier, there are no real investigative reporters covering Templeton. We should use your skills in the time we have before you get assigned to covering the school board again."

She understood a putdown when she heard one, but he appeared to be complimenting her at the same time. His backhand was formidable. His serve, not so much.

"Gee. And at first I thought you were flirting with me."

"Honey, if I thought flirting worked, I'd have done it years ago. But I learned even longer ago pretty newspaper reporters never bite. I guess it's the pressure of being so damned hot that you can't let your guard down for a moment."

"You're still doing it."

"What's wrong? Can't take a compliment?"

"I just thought—"

"You just thought an old guy like me, old enough to be your dad, would hop in the sack with you? Lady, I have two daughters almost as young as you are. I always wonder why a woman can't just take a compliment from a man and accept there's no ulterior motive."

"I'm sorry."

"Yeah, well."

She kicked herself. She'd read him wrong. She needed to be more careful lest she piss off her only potential source at the moment.

"You're good," Grant said. "You probably should be on the national beat. And right now, I need an investigative reporter. You're all I got." He paused for a moment and looked into her eyes.

She felt as if he was measuring her up. But for once, a man's scan did not go below her chin. Maybe she could like this guy.

"Look," he said, "you're not stupid. Your work shows that. So, I need to be up front with you. I can't stand Templeton. I've been in politics for more than two decades. It's all about winning, and we needed Templeton so Crofton could win. We used him. That's all it was. Had last night not happened, we'd have locked him up in his cage for the next four years. Now I fear we've unleashed a monster. I love this country, and this guy is going to be a disaster."

"What do you mean?" she asked.

"He's unfit. He's going senile for Christ's sake. In fact, it's much worse than that. He's in the beginning stages of Alzheimer's disease."

"You're kidding. How can you say that?"

"I was on the team to interview him for the vice presidency last summer. It was pretty clear he wasn't right, but I'm no psychologist. But I know someone who is. A friend I went to college with. Actually, she's a psychiatrist in Idaho. So I called her and asked if she could help. I explained I'd insert her into the campaign as a speechwriter for Templeton so she could observe his behavior up close and have an excuse to have extensive conversations with him. She'd never been in politics before, but I knew she could write. She used to correct some of my papers in college—and I was the English and journalism major.

"So we agreed to keep her profession quiet and she'd report secretly back to me. So many people were being hired for the campaign last August, no one even vetted my friend. My recommendation was good enough."

Tish watched Grant closely, chomping away and talking. He was totally caught up in his story.

"My friend spent all of September examining him. In her role as speechwriter, she could ask Templeton questions about his opinions. She traveled with him on the campaign plane, watched him wolf down fast-food burgers, and listened carefully to his conversations. They actually became friends and would joke around together. Templeton invited her to play golf with him at one of his courses. Can you imagine a candidate for vice president taking the weekend off late in the campaign to play golf? Templeton is a lazy bastard, and he could care less about policy. He'd throw a few simplistic criticisms about Washington out to the crowds when he spoke, and they ate it up. He refused to do any more than that. No intellectual heft. No curiosity. No mental muscle put into it.

"Of course his real motivation in inviting her to play golf was to make a pass at her. Leigh told me—that's her name, Leigh Child—she told me she handled it well and let his ego keep its dignity. She said he wasn't smooth at all. Kind of a bull in a china shop. Almost childish, she said.

"But then you have to see Leigh to understand. She'd make even an impertinent guy like Templeton turn blubbery. She's a real babe. Legs up to here." He raised his flattened palm high above the table and kept going. "And a body that only God could sculpt. Blonde. Beautiful face. The whole package. She's forty, and men still fall at her feet. I think that's why she never married. She can still have any man she wants.

"But I'm getting off subject. What I'm trying to say is Templeton is a hound dog. He'll chase any pretty skirt that prances within barking distance. He feels he's entitled. I think he sees Leigh as a challenge. She sees that and has decided it is to her advantage to play coy. That's why he's still attracted to her."

"But he's married," said Tish.

"So? This is a man who has an incredible sense of entitlement to absolutely everything. He has a gorgeous wife, and I understand from staffers she is quite nice. But that doesn't stop him from cheating on her. She's little more than arm candy to him. Everyone in his orbit is disposable."

Grant was painting a picture of Templeton Tish had never imagined. She had heard tidbits about his lack of attention to detail and some of his boorish ways, and she had even experienced them first hand this morning. But she had no idea he was such an egotist. Yet, she knew people who run for president must have extremely healthy views of themselves. So she couldn't really hold that against him. But the cheating. That bothered her.

"So anyway," he continued, "Leigh would draft him an entire speech, and Templeton might remember a few catchphrases, and then wing it at the next campaign stop. He had no interest in other people's opinions or words. Only his own."

"So how does a man like that become so successful?" Tish asked.

"That's the question I asked. And my friend came back with the stunning answer. Templeton had a great mind for business at one time. But no more. As I said earlier, he is in the first stages of Alzheimer's disease. He's losing his mind. But at this stage, he is still able to keep most of it covered up."

"I don't understand," said Tish. She took a sip of her soda water and set it back down on the dark wooden tabletop. She noticed someone's initials carved into the surface.

"The way Leigh explained it to me was to think of a spiderweb growing inside your brain. Everything it touches—every neuron—dies. However, before any dementia becomes noticeable, your brain manages to do a work-around. Think of it as an electric grid in a big city. If one power line goes down serving your city block, no biggie. Another line carries the electricity to your block. But if every line leading to your block eventually goes down, the entire block goes dark. All the lines to the city blocks in Templeton's brain have not yet gone dark. So he can still compensate. He can still function. But it's only a matter of time. And this man with half a good brain left will have access to our nuclear codes."

Tish suddenly felt cold and rubbed her arms. She was way out of her league.

Grant kept talking. "My psychiatrist friend even went back and pulled old television interviews with Templeton and played them side by side with recent ones. Leigh told me Templeton's vocabulary is a fraction of what it was a decade ago. That's an early sign of dementia. Victims repeat themselves. He uses the same words over and over again. He locks in on them and can't find others to express his thoughts. He's kept his superlatives—the greatest, the worst—all of that, but he's lost his nuance. He has the vocabulary of a blunt object.

"And he's angry. Deep down he knows something is wrong. His anger will get worse, Leigh says. That's what happens to Alzheimer's patients when they realize something is wrong, and they can't vocalize or process the way they used to. They get frustrated because they can't cope."

"Making decisions based on anger can't be good," said Tish.

"He either loves you or he hates you," Grant said. "His emotional range is this big." Grant held his thumb and forefinger an inch apart. "His attention span is just as long. Leigh also said he struggles with attention deficit disorder. The guy's a mental mess."

"I'm amazed he has been able to cover it up for so long," Tish said.

"You have to be around the guy a lot to see all the signs. Like I said, he can still hide it so the average Joe doesn't catch on." Grant paused and looked at his new beer that had arrived while he was talking. He was about to lift it and then seemed to think better of it. "Leigh's mother died at the end of October, so she left the campaign. She didn't return. I sent her a card, but I haven't reached out to her since. You know. End of the campaign. Everybody's working twenty-four seven."

"Who knows about this?"

"About Templeton's dementia?"

Tish nodded.

"I told Crofton and our campaign manager. Well, I told Crofton, so that means our campaign manager knows. Bedtime conversation, I'm sure. Crofton told me to keep it strictly confidential. The last thing we needed was for the world to know a mental case was on the party ticket."

Tish flinched at Grant's belittling language.

"And besides," he continued, "we all thought we'd lose. By October, as the race tightened a little, we just wanted to save face and have everyone think we ran a respectable campaign. We never dreamed this would happen. On the outside chance Crofton somehow performed a miracle, we figured we could deal with Templeton and have him eventually removed."

"Why tell me this?"

"I need someone to get that story out, and you appear to be the only one available right now. Sorry. Didn't mean that to come out the way it did. Like I said, you've impressed me. I need someone who isn't jaded to look at this seriously. We're in big shit, and we need to deal with it. I'm in no position. I have no cred with Templeton. I was a Crofton person. Believe me, he will surround himself with his own people, whoever they turn out to be."

"But you said this was off the record."

"Background is what I said. You can use the information. You just can't tie me to your story. I seriously doubt I will have a job in the new administration, but I need to keep my options open. At a meeting this morning Templeton told both his and Crofton's campaign staffs that job preferences would go to his staff first, but there were jobs for everybody if they wanted one."

"What you've told me is extraordinary." Tish was bewildered. She needed time to assess everything he had dumped on her. "If all of this is true, we have an incapacitated president with the mental ability of what? A fourteen-year-old? And the ability to wage a world war?"

"Precisely. See why I need your help?" Grant finished his beer and slapped his mug on the table. He looked like a man needing to burp but couldn't. This time, he did not look around the restaurant to wave down the waiter.

"But how does anyone prove any of this?" Tish asked. "I mean everyone is so sensitive these days about mental health and mental deficiencies."

"I didn't say it would be easy. But you seem to have more ability to find the truth than those nattering nabobs who cover and comment on the campaigns these days. To them it's nothing more than a souped-up horse race. It has nothing to do with issues or even mental appropriateness. It's headlines and ratings."

She hated it when people made broadsides against the press. But she knew it was partially true, but not so for the good practitioners—newspapers like hers.

"Can I meet your psychiatrist friend?"

"I can try to reach her, but I'm not sure she will talk. I doubt seriously she would go on the record with anything. It could mean her license. The ethics of her profession not only limit what she can say, but her conduct when treating a patient."

"Hasn't she already crossed that line analyzing Templeton without his knowledge?" Tish wondered how she'd ever get the story without Leigh Child's help.

"Remember, she's not treating him. She's examining him for her own curiosity and mine. Nothing more. The minute she goes public with a diagnosis, she could face all types of professional sanctions." Grant flexed his fingers as he talked, first tightening them and then letting them loose as if from stiffness or arthritis.

"Still, I need to talk with her," Tish insisted. "Without her help, there probably is no story." She decided to press him for help. She saw no other way to go after the story.

Grant hesitated. "I can make a phone call. I believe she's in South Carolina."

"I thought you said she was in Idaho."

"Duh. That doesn't mean her mother was."

Okay. She deserved that. She'd spoken before she'd thought. She found herself doing that too often lately.

"I'll try to speak to her to see if she will come back. I'm really scared what Templeton might do. I'm thinking if I can woo Leigh to take a White House job, we can observe the president's state of mind from the inside."

"You'd do that?"

"You're damned right I would. No one understands how grave this is but Crofton's campaign manager, me, and now you. I'm taking one hell of a risk confiding in you."

VII

When Tish first saw the store clerk, she effused aloofness. Meryl must be right. Her clothes must not make a very good impression. Really though, they couldn't be that bad. Maybe it was Tish herself. It wouldn't be the first time she was prejudged by her skin tone. So she turned immediately to the designer racks and started picking through clothes. It was like someone had turned up the thermostat.

Tish found a sweater, three blouses—two designer—a few pairs of slacks, two jackets, a skirt, and some expensive scarves that she could coordinate to quickly change her look. She turned before the dressing room mirror, and the designer stuff looked good on her. She didn't know how long she was going to be in New York, so she needed to be able to mix and match to extend her wardrobe. She even picked up some sexy lingerie. Tom would like that.

In all, she'd spent more than $1,800. Worrying about what her boss might think hadn't entered her mind. Her thoughts were elsewhere. She couldn't get her conversation with Grant out of her head. Why did he confide in her? Surely he knew plenty of investigative reporters, even if they weren't covering the Templeton campaign. They would show up in droves in New York now that Crofton had been assassinated.

Grant didn't know her. She knew she had a decent reporting history, but she knew it was thin by comparison with more seasoned reporters. No national reporting experience except for last night, and that didn't really prove anything. It hadn't been difficult. She'd just reported the facts. She'd really done very little reporting—just watching Tom's video.

In fact, because of her lack of knowledge of the technology, her reporting efforts had failed miserably. She'd lost her interview with Crofton's press secretary because of dead batteries.

Yet it was her efforts during the evening that led the news. She was a bit flabbergasted that it had been so easy, not like one of her long investigations she had conducted in her former newspaper job. She felt unworthy. She was getting more recognition than she deserved. And somehow she had caught Grant's attention. Why?

He didn't know her. Maybe that was it. She stood at the cashier's counter, holding the skirt she wanted to buy. Grant was playing this safe. No one could connect them. That explained the meeting at the bar where no one would ever see them.

Then she had another thought. Could he be setting her up? Could he be using her as a patsy for some bigger scheme? If she wrote a story exposing Templeton as unfit, what then? Who would become the next president? Or would Templeton remain in office?

"Ma'am?"

Tish looked up. The clerk had rung up everything but the skirt in her hands.

"Oh, sorry," she said. Tish handed the woman the garment. She was becoming obsessed. No, she was being ridiculous. She didn't want to become one of those journalists who found a conspiracy around every corner. This was happening in real time. Grant had confided in her something that last night's serendipity had set in motion. She just happened to be in the right place at the right time. That's all.

She thought about the investigation into Crofton's murder. She'd been out of touch with any media all afternoon. It was dark when she had left the bar and even darker now on this moonless night. It had been a long day and she decided to rest her eyes and take a taxi back to Tom's apartment. The conspiracy theories, no doubt, would start soon. She needed to rest her brain for now. This was all getting too complicated too quickly.

VIII

When Tish opened the door to Tom's apartment, she found him at the table sitting with the two FBI agents—the real agents.

"Where have you been?" Tom asked.

The agents stared at her and she at them and then she looked back to Tom. "I told you I was going shopping." She lifted her bags flashing the department store logo.

"You left your phone," Tom said. "I tried to reach you."

"Sorry. Didn't mean to." But she knew full well she had. One of the conditions Jim Grant had demanded was she leave her phone at home. He had even rummaged through her purse when she arrived assuring she hadn't brought it with her. Only after their conversation had she realized how careful he had been. She had been on the subway heading to the department store when it had dawned on her Grant may have been worried that someone might try to track her phone via GPS. Why? Or maybe he feared she would record their conversation. But why?

Answers would have to wait.

She looked back at the FBI agents. "What do you want?"

The female agent, Kathy Mueller, stood and waved to one of the kitchen table chairs. "We've just been discussing last night. We're hoping you might have seen something and maybe hadn't realized its importance. That's all."

"We've been through all this," Tish protested.

"They identified the fake FBI agents," Tom said. "They're Russian agents."

"What? Who?" she asked. "Why appear as FBI agents and take a copy of your video?"

Mueller interrupted. "Obviously, there may be something on that video to give us a clue to the murderer of the president-elect."

"It gets even better," Tom said. "CNN reported about a half hour ago that the FBI is investigating Crofton's Republican opponent, Senator Steve Berry. They're saying he might have had Crofton assassinated."

"That's unbelievable."

"Remember his statement about unleashing the so-called 'Second Amendment people' on her? That's what they're looking at."

"Oh, that's silly," said Tish. "It was just political thunder. Everybody knows that."

"I guess it proves you gotta watch your mouth when campaigning," Tom said.

"We're taking everything seriously," Agent Mueller said. "That's why we're here."

"They asked me to walk through last night again," Tom said. "I told them everything I know about the remote camera next to me. And they want to talk to you too. That's why I was trying to reach you, only to hear your phone ring back in the bedroom."

"The Russian agents, as you know from Tom's video, were in the crowd last night," said Mueller. "We have compiled videos from a number of cameramen and found they were watching you and several other individuals at the party."

"Me? Why me?"

"That's what we'd like to know."

"I have no idea. I wasn't even supposed to be there." She looked over at Tom. "I assume Tom told you I was pitching in when he lost his freelance reporter. Mistaken identity maybe? Or was it because of what I was doing there? Where I was standing maybe?"

"Can you think of any reason why they showed interest in you?" Mueller asked. She turned and looked at her partner, whose expression was bewilderment.

"The closest I've ever come to anything Russian was a one-semester class in Russian politics when I was in college," said Tish. "I've never even been there. I took an Italian geography class too. But I doubt that helps."

"Let's talk about last night," Mueller said. "Look at these photos." She handed her Tom's stills showing the crowd. Circled in the photos were the two agents she had met passing themselves off as FBI agents. "You see. They are staring at you."

"I've got a microphone in my hand interviewing Crofton's press secretary," Tish said. "I didn't even notice them."

"We find it interesting that the interview was never recorded—at least the audio wasn't."

"Yeah, well, Tom's not too keen on that either. You can thank my ineptness with broadcasting equipment. I'm a print reporter. I use a notebook not a microphone. But we finally got it figured out."

"Just in time for the assassination," Mueller said.

"And just what are you insinuating?" Tom asked. "You think our technical foul-up was deliberate?"

"Convenient."

"Convenient for what? I could have made more money with that interview."

"Convenient because you have no earlier video or sound of the remote camera set up right next to you. You said it was already there when you arrived. Your video and the sound you recorded of the remote are the only evidence we have of the device prior to the assassination. No other videographers picked it up."

"Accuse them of something. Don't accuse me," Tom shot back.

"We're not accusing you of anything. But if you have any more information you wish to share, we'd like to know it."

"I've cooperated fully. I think it's time you both leave."

Tish had never seen Tom so indignant.

"We've done nothing wrong." He was almost yelling. "In fact, we've both bent over backward to cooperate. You don't come into my home and question my integrity."

Tom stood from the table and abruptly shoved his chair back with his legs.

"I think you're right. We should talk another time," Mueller said. The agents stood, thanked them for their cooperation, and quickly left without shaking hands.

After Tom closed the door behind them, he turned to Tish. "What the hell?"

Tish shook her head. "I'm stunned. They suspect us of some kind of collusion. I don't get it. We've done nothing but try and help."

Tom walked to the refrigerator and pulled out a beer. He grabbed an open bottle of wine off the counter and offered her a glass. She thought it was a good idea.

They sat at the table instead of the couch where they usually sat with a drink.

"I'm totally confused about what's going on," Tom said.

Tish swirled the wine in her glass longer than she should have and finally took a drink. She was clueless too.

IX

Derrick Templeton was up late, as he always was. He didn't need much sleep. His butler had already set out on his gilded dining room table his diet soda and hamburger and fries from the fast-food restaurant on the first floor. Templeton thumbed through the New York tabloids and *Wall Street Journal* and eyed the cable news shows. His wife, Melinda, was sleeping.

He stood and walked over to the window and looked out from the top of Templeton Tower over the darkened Manhattan skyline. This city had been his for decades. Now he owned the world. He couldn't believe it. He had never thought he'd win. He had run for vice president because it would help his businesses. He had grown richer in recent years selling the rights to his name. The campaign was supposed to make his brand priceless and expand his empire. Now what was he supposed to do? He hadn't planned ahead.

Now his only plan was to leave tomorrow for some R&R at his Florida estate. He'd promised Melinda they would go to Florida immediately after the election.

Without a doubt she was the best-looking partner he had ever had. He loved beautiful things, and she was a former international model. She had competed as Miss Ukraine in one of his beauty contests and he made sure she won. He asked her out shortly after.

Neither knew what was coming next. The first sign of the future was the extra security at his front door and Secret Service agents inside his penthouse.

"Sir."

Templeton turned from his view at the sound of a Secret Service agent.

"Please step back from the window. It's not bulletproof."

Wow, thought Templeton. He was that important now. He was liking this.

"Bulletproof panels should be delivered tomorrow," his guard said.

Templeton grabbed his cell phone and hit the son-in-law key. "Harold, you asleep? We need to talk. Grab Vanna too. Fifteen minutes. In the penthouse."

Harold and his daughter were his two top lieutenants—both in business and in the campaign. He sipped his soda and went back to eyeing his shows and reading the tabloids. They were lamenting Crofton's death and saying Templeton had big shoes to fill. Really? Her shoes? She had accomplished nothing. Look at the empire he had built. He was the accomplished one. And he'd make sure the world knew it too. He would move quickly, like he always did. That was his world—fast and furious. He loved the pace.

Harold and Vanna arrived, both in skinny jeans and sneakers. Vanna had on no makeup and appeared to have barely combed her hair. Harold's white shirt was wrinkled and he looked like he needed a shower. Templeton didn't like what he saw. He always wanted his family looking great. Really great.

"Where do we go from here?" Templeton asked.

"Derrick, I think we first have to deal with Crofton's death," said Harold. "It's a ritual. Visit the family. Go through the whole funeral thing. I know you weren't close to her, but for public appearances, let's get that out of the way. There's got to be some period of mourning."

"Mourning? I'm celebrating." Templeton started to laugh.

"Let's watch that kind of talk," said Harold. "And maybe you shouldn't fly to Florida tomorrow. It might look bad when we will soon bury your running mate."

"Screw that. We're going to the Palace. I promised Melinda. It's my home just as much as this is. Doesn't matter where we are staying. We can always fly to wherever they bury the bitch."

"You realize you can no longer fly on your 727. The government will provide you an aircraft," Vanna said.

"Great. Look at the money we'll save. Let them know we leave tomorrow morning for Florida. And one of the Secret Service agents said they will equip the penthouse with bulletproof windows tomorrow. Will they do that in Florida too?"

"I suppose so," Harold said. "I'll talk to the Secret Service."

"Let's get this out of the way, as quickly as you said. Bury the bitch. What I do for my country—man—this is a great day. The best." Templeton looked around the room. His decorator had filled it with all this French stuff. He loved this room with all its mirrors and gold. The furniture wasn't so comfortable, but then he never sat down for long.

Then Vanna spoke. "Daddy, we need to put together a transition team. You've got to create a new government. Maybe we should use Crofton's team."

"Screw her. Let's put our own team together," Templeton said.

"But we'd be starting from zero," said Harold.

Templeton looked at him. What was he thinking? No way was he using Crofton's staff. They loved her, not him. "Doesn't matter. I know people."

"Okay. But then we need to address the most important appointments you need for your new administration," Harold said. "The secretary of state, the attorney general, secretary of defense, secretary of the treasury and your chief of staff."

"Piece of cake. I have lots of friends who have lots of money who will be willing to serve. And we have two months to do it. Lots of time." Templeton could feel himself getting bored.

"And then we need to address the business," Harold said.

"What about the business?" Templeton perked up.

"You've got to give it up. History dictates you divest yourself of your business holdings so you have no conflict of interest."

"Nuts to that. I've built a multi-billion-dollar empire. I'm not giving that up. Screw history. Figure it out. Call my lawyers. I'm not giving up my business for anybody. Not even to be president. They can't make me."

"I'll look into it," Vanna said.

"Good. Next," Templeton said.

The three talked for another twenty minutes, which was all Templeton could take before he kicked them out. God, he hated details. He was the visionary and he had a grand one. The world was going to see just how grand. He was going to be a great president—the greatest ever.

X

"Have we missed anything?" Tish asked, sipping on her wine. It was late and she was ready for bed. She looked across the table at Tom. He was still fiddling with his laptop, looking again at the footage from election night.

"I don't know. I've looked at this a hundred times. I see the two Russians in the background, maybe fifteen feet directly behind you when you were trying to get your microphone fixed. The FBI agents are wrong. The Russians aren't paying any more attention to you than anyone else. I think those agents were just probing. I guess that's their job."

"That's a relief," Tish said.

"I remember I couldn't hear you then because my headphone jack wasn't fully plugged in. After I fixed that, we could both hear each other. No, before that, I plugged in my shotgun mike," he said as he continued to stare at his computer screen.

"What does that do?" Tish asked. She'd never heard of a shotgun mike before.

"It can pick up sound from across the room. I just point it at you. That's how I could hear you so I could explain how to replace your batteries in your microphone. Obviously, I couldn't hear you through your powerless remote mike. I put your mike on one track and the shotgun on another."

Tish grabbed his arm, and he turned to her. "Did you record what your shotgun mike picked up?" she asked.

He was silent. Thinking. He turned to his computer again.

"What?" asked Tish.

"I must have. It's got to be on another track. I totally forgot about it. I just used the audio from your mike during the video I sold to everyone. You were on the whole time after you exchanged the batteries."

He began typing furiously. "The other track should be right here." He hit a key, and the screen showed some serious vertical lines. "I've got it."

He hit another key and suddenly sound flowed from his remote speakers.

"Now let me synch it with the video." He hit more keys. "Here we go."

She watched the screen over Tom's shoulder and saw the Russians in the background, but she could not make out what they were saying.

"Hang on. I can filter some of this," Tom said. He typed on several keys. And then more. He repeated the process a couple of times and moved his curser around the screen. "This is a shotgun mike, so the ambient sound is limited to what is directly in its path. So it shouldn't be too difficult to filter out any superfluous sound."

Tish didn't understand any of it. All she saw was a bunch of lines and numbers.

He zoomed in on the Russians' faces. "Now listen carefully. Try to match the sound to their lips. You hear that?"

"I can hear something, but I'm not sure what it is."

He flipped to another screen and looked at his audio board. "There," he said, pointing a finger at some lines on the screen. He punched more keys, and several lines disappeared. "Let's listen to this. I'll sync it to the video again."

"Is it ready?" came a voice from the speakers. "Anatoly says all is ready. He's in the van. The remote's working. Everything is set."

"Quiet you fool. Stay here," came another voice. "We don't want to be near it."

"Oh my God," said Tish. "They're talking about that camera-weapon thing."

"I think you're right," Tom said.

"Is there any more?"

Tom searched the lines on the screen again. Tish had no idea what he was looking for.

"I think that's all."

"Was this on the recording you gave the Russians?"

"Like I said, I forgot about it. It's a separate track. This is the only copy."

"Oh, thank God," she said.

"What are you talking about?"

"Don't you see? That's what the Russians were looking for. Any evidence that shows their culpability. Neither they, nor the FBI, know you have evidence tying the two Russians to the assassination. You've got to get this to the FBI."

"You mean the guys who just accused us of colluding with killers? I think I'd reconsider that. Don't you think this will give them the evidence they need to accuse us of covering up?"

"Tell them the truth," Tish urged.

Tom looked at her like she was crazy.

XI

It was late when Jim Grant's call to his old friend Leigh Child went to voicemail. He asked her to call him immediately. It was urgent. Thirty minutes later his phone rang.

"What's up Jimbo?" Child said, using his pet name from college.

"I need you to talk to a reporter about Templeton."

"Not a good idea. I just got a call from his people. They want me to work for him in the White House."

"You're considering it?"

Grant was sitting on his hotel room bed in his underwear. Light from the two bedside lamps caught the voluptuous profile of the alluring campaign volunteer. She had been flirting with him for weeks and now sat naked at the foot of the bed. She was ready and looked frustrated and almost young enough to be his daughter.

He covered his phone with his hand and whispered, "I need to take this."

She frowned and looked down at her nakedness as if she were making an offering. Then she looked up and flipped him the bird.

He stood and walked into the bathroom and closed the door.

"Damn right I'm thinking about working there," Leigh said. "He shouldn't be elected dogcatcher or even local alderman. The guy's mentally unfit. We need to surround him with enough good people to stop him from doing some serious damage."

"Then why not talk to my friend? She's a reporter. Go public with what you know?"

"I'm a doctor for crying out loud. I have an oath to uphold."

"But you just said he's a danger to others."

"That's my medical opinion—made after an examination done without the patient's consent. It won't hold up anywhere."

"But if you work in the White House, you'll be vetted. They'll find out you're a shrink." Grant couldn't hide his concern.

"So. That doesn't disqualify me. You think he's got any idea I've got a book of notes an inch thick on his demeanor? You need to understand he's delusional. He's a narcissist. He's got an ego the size of Mount Rushmore and thinks his mug belongs there. If he learns I have a medical background, it won't make any difference to him. He won't be threatened. In fact, it could work in my favor. It will likely make him yearn even more to get in my pants."

"Does he want you to write speeches again?" Jim sat on the edge of the tub and glanced at himself in the mirror on the back of the bathroom door. He looked like he hadn't slept in a week, which was close to the truth.

"Yes and no. Right now I have to make him sound sympathetic to Crofton and her family. His communications chief wants help putting out a press statement. But if that keeps me in his inner circle, so be it. This one is damage control. He told some reporter he'd do a better job than Crofton as president. He's dangerous off the cuff."

"That's the reporter I want you to talk to."

"Is she the one everyone was quoting election night?"

"The same," said Grant.

"I don't know." She paused. "Not sure what my new role will be. What Templeton really needs is someone to talk to, to confide in. The man is lonely. He's really insecure about his lack of knowledge, and he covers it up by bullying people. He refuses to learn more not because he doesn't want to, but because he can't. He needs a friend like me who's going to be sympathetic. I'm like one of the family, only less so because I have no agenda, at least not one he's aware of.

"His son-in-law Harold called me," she continued. "He sounded desperate. Wants me to meet him in Florida in three or four days to hold Templeton's hand. Look, I gotta go."

"Before you go to Florida, come to New York and talk to this woman privately."

"I'll think about it, but I can't talk about this publicly. I'd never work again."

"I get that," Jim said. He hung up and thought about the conversation. So Templeton was going to the Palace in Florida for a vacation. Then he heard noise outside his door. Oh shit. He'd left her on the bed.

He grabbed the bathroom door and swung it open. She was gone. He knew he shouldn't have let her seduce him. She was a campaign volunteer. Now he was paying the price.

He looked around the room. Where were his clothes? He checked the closet. She'd taken them all. He shook his head.

He stepped over to the bed and pulled back the covers and nearly fell on the mattress. He was too exhausted to care anymore.

XII

Tish wanted to make love. She was wound tight from the day's events. A nice round of sex would expel her pent-up anxieties. She took off her makeup, scrubbed her face and slipped on her sexy new lingerie. Tom wouldn't know what hit him tonight. She smiled in the mirror at the thought.

She turned off the bathroom light and entered the darkened bedroom.

Tom was snoring.

Her body slumped and desire drained from her being. She turned to the bureau and stripped, and stuffed her new lingerie in the drawer Tom reserved for her. She crawled in bed beside him.

She looked at Tom, with his bare back to her, intermittently groaning and snoring. She wrapped an arm around him and spooned, feeling the warmth of his body against her own.

She had wondered early on in their relationship how it might work out—a biracial girl with an Irish Catholic man. And then he had complicated it when he'd told her his mother's maiden name was Bernstein. He was also Jewish. It had made her laugh. A Jew, an Irishman, an African American, and a Western European. All they needed to do was walk into a bar together and wait for the punch line.

They were quite the modern mix.

She was happy to be able to spend some extra days with him in New York, and he had been thrilled at the news she would stay longer. He was the first white man she had ever gotten serious enough about to have sex with. She had dated plenty of white guys, but they could never quite get over her multiracial roots. She was different, she had to admit, what with one foot in the African-American community and one in white America. She felt comfortable in both but not completely accepted by either.

She liked that Tom looked at her for who she was. He'd admitted he hadn't considered her light brown skin color when he first met her. Except for her natural black curls, he told her she could be mistaken for any white woman with a deep tan. She wasn't sure how to take that. But what she did like was when Tom had said he fell for her because she was smart and beautiful. She liked that he had first mentioned her brain, although she didn't mind at all that he thought she was hot. Coming from him—and not Derrick Templeton—it was flattering.

When she'd pressed him, he'd acknowledged he had never dated a black woman before and promptly reminded her he wasn't now. Well, he had her there. Sort of. It only reminded her of her complicated heritage. And then he had added he'd dated a woman once who previously had a two-year affair with another woman.

Relationships, he said, were based on today's flavor, not one's history or stereotype. She liked the sound of that, but she didn't want to be the flavor of the month. She was starting to think more about a lifetime.

She felt his nipple and her fingers massaged his chest. She thought how ironic. If he were awake, it would be the other way around. But tonight, she consoled herself knowing he desperately needed rest.

It bothered her that he wasn't willing to give the other track of audio to the FBI. For some reason, he didn't trust them. Wouldn't they understand if he told them the truth and that he had forgotten all about it? After all, when they went back through his video and found the two Russians in the crowd and made stills, the agents were more than grateful to get the information. They hadn't questioned his motives then.

She understood an investigation was like peeling the layers of an onion. She'd done it many times in her short journalism career and found the experience exhilarating. And that, she realized, was the difference between them. Tom was more artistic, although very technically astute, as she had found with his ability to enhance the video and audio on his laptop. She viewed herself, though, as more firmly grounded in hard facts than he was.

Still, she had to admit to her own artistic proclivity. Perhaps that's what attracted her to Tom. It was genetic and something she couldn't avoid since her dad was a fairly successful artist back in DC. But it was her late mom who had grounded her in the real world, who had taught her about her African heritage. She hadn't known much else. Her dad was an only child and both of his parents had died before she was born. The only family she knew was from her mom's side, where a dozen cousins and lots of aunts and uncles were scattered about, many of them in Washington.

Yet she had grown up in what she came to realize was a white household. Nearly all her childhood friends had been white or the children of foreign diplomats. Few blacks had attended her high school. Growing up in Chevy Chase gave her little choice. There had been few African Americans in her neighborhood and yet her mother had insisted on living there. When she was older and in college, Tish had learned her mother had regretted it. As a teenager she had wanted to spend more time hanging out with her girlfriends, but her mother had started pushing her to spend Sundays with her cousins. Now she understood why.

After her mom died during her sophomore year, her dad moved to Old Town Alexandria and set up shop in the old Torpedo Factory to be near other artists, he said. But she thought it was more about not being able to live in their old home without Mom. He was so heartbroken he couldn't even look at the walls after the cancer consumed her. Tish had mourned too, but not like her dad.

She felt Tom's nipple again and then rolled away and felt her own. Funny. Had she not had breasts they would feel the same. She had read once how men and women start out exactly alike as fetuses. It is only after their DNA kicked in and the fetus began to grow that sexual characteristics are distinguishable. She loved the idea that she shared ninety percent of her being with this precious man.

The thought made her feel closer to him, until he interrupted her with a grunt and loud snore. Well, sometimes too close. She turned away and pulled the pillow over her head and tried to concentrate on what she had learned since the assassination.

She needed to talk to Templeton's speechwriter. She wondered if Grant would actually make the ask. She'd follow up in the morning. And what about the FBI and Tom's other audio track? She needed to talk him into giving them a copy. She didn't understand his reluctance. Was he just angry with them or was there something else there she hadn't seen?

She pulled the pillow off her head and rolled over to look at him again. She knew him, but she didn't understand this about him. Maybe she needed to rethink their relationship. Was she going too fast? What was she not seeing?

Maybe he was just tired. That was it. He was just exhausted from being up nearly forty-eight hours straight. He would make more sense in the morning.

And then she thought of something else. Tom had been with the FBI when she'd gotten back to the apartment. What had been said before she'd arrived? That must be the key to this. Something the FBI had said to Tom spooked him. She feared she'd stay awake all night trying to figure it out. Instead, she promised herself she would deal with it in the morning.

She rolled over again and pulled the pillow over her head. It was her turn to fall asleep.

XIII

Mikhail Usmanov closed the door of his condominium directly beneath Derrick Templeton's massive two-floor penthouse. More than a dozen years ago, back when he still had hair, Usmanov had purchased his condo and four others, buying the entire twenty-seventh floor of Derrick Templeton's building. At the time, Usmanov liked to think he cut a dashing figure. He needed to launder some dirty cash and get it out of Russia quickly to finance his taste for expensive American women, beluga caviar and European cars. He hadn't been able to trust the Russian banks and he certainly didn't trust Vladimir Platkin, the new president. Both would have taken a hefty portion of his hard-earned wealth if they'd had half a chance.

He wasn't exactly innocent himself. He had stolen it after Gorbachev's perestroika had spread throughout the former Soviet Union. It had been easy pickings for savvy party officials as they took for their own the newly privatized state machinery and transformed it into their own private fortunes.

They had unofficially become the Russian Mafia. And like the Mafia, riches came with a price. Russian President Platkin was better organized today than long ago and now took a cut of all of Usmanov's deals. Even the cash Usmanov had earlier laundered through purchasing this floor of condos, was fair game. In return for sharing his riches with Platkin, Usmanov had no worries about walking down Fifth Avenue one day and looking over his shoulder at a Russian assassin. It may not have been a fair deal, but he could make a convincing argument it was a deal worth making.

It was rumored Platkin, who had managed to escape a corruption probe early in his political career, was now the richest leader in the world thanks to skimming off everyone else's pile. He was the glue that held the Mafia in check and the proletariat at bay. We all swim or drown together, Platkin had reminded them. Platkin? Swim? Not on your life. Today he walked on water—Russian water, anyway.

And one of the five condominiums in Templeton Tower proved it. Platkin bought it from Usmanov through a series of offshore shell corporations. Usmanov was actually eager at the time to make the deal. It was a time when he needed some clean cash. His weakness for American women was more expensive than he had anticipated.

Usmanov grinned at the irony of the Russian prime minister, an official enemy of the United States, was not only supporting the president-elect, but he was his neighbor.

Shell companies were Usmanov's MO. Separate shell companies owned each of his condos in Templeton Tower. Templeton Tower was one of only two condominium buildings in Manhattan that allowed buyers to hide their ownership in corporate shells. Yet now government officials were trying to pass laws to disclose the true owners. He knew they would never figure it out. The ownership trail was just too complicated. He made sure of that.

He remembered when he had first approached Templeton about purchasing a condo the billionaire seemed pleased. When he'd understood Usmanov wanted to purchase an entire floor, Templeton had been beside himself. And he never asked where the money came from. It had been an unspoken understanding between two savvy businesspeople. No questions. Just show me the money.

When it became clear Templeton was running for president, Usmanov had begun installing listening devices in his properties to monitor the candidate's private life one floor above. It was not like he'd thought Templeton stood a chance of winning, but he had known having an important American billionaire in his pocket could someday prove useful. And if he were going to install the devices, he had better do it early. Just in case. He would have never gotten this far amassing his own wealth by not being prepared.

So nearly two years ago, a team of Russian technicians had entered the building and begun their work. And some eight months later, Templeton had somehow found himself in second place in the delegate race for the Democratic nomination. He'd even garnered Secret Service protection.

Templeton eventually lost to Crofton and had joined the party ticket. That's when Russian oligarch Ivan Domnin appeared, almost out of nowhere. Usmanov had thought they were taking an unnecessary risk. Domnin had public ties to the Kremlin and a good working relationship with Platkin. If the Americans didn't know about his connection, they soon would. There had been little subtlety about it. Domnin was jeopardizing his operation. It was Domnin's idea to show up at the Crofton party on election night. Usmanov had accompanied him to assure he didn't do anything stupid.

Over the decade, Templeton and Usmanov had become friendly and discussed business on numerous occasions. He had even helped Templeton reach out to Russian oligarchs when his Atlantic City casinos had been disintegrating. Templeton had eventually declared bankruptcy for three of his corporations and it had not been clear then if he would ever recover.

Instead he had quickly made a miraculous financial rebound. No one could figure out how, even when he had written a book bragging about it. Usmanov had read a translation and realized the book was all lies. Usmanov had known the source of all of Templeton's liquidity to pay his bills—more than $1 billion—was from his Russian friends. He'd help set it up. Platkin made it clear he wanted Templeton to remain viable. But now, after all the Russian refinancings and new loans, the bill was coming due quickly. It put Usmanov in an enviable position. The next president of the United States was in his debt. Big time.

Usmanov had learned over the years that Templeton was a risk junky. He made outrageous claims and took unfathomable risks. But he always fashioned his deals so if they went south, Templeton still profited. The guy was a genius, thought Usmanov. But he knew better than to ever go into business with him. After Templeton bragged to him one evening over drinks in the penthouse how he had taken some contractors to the cleaners on one of his deals, Usmanov had contacted his Manhattan attorneys and had them re-read his condo sales contracts. He'd take no chances with Templeton. The lawyers had assured him the sales were solid.

So when he'd orchestrated the deals with the Russian Mafia, Usmanov had made it very clear to Templeton these were loans with ties to people who would not accept nonpayment. Templeton might do that with his American banks, but not with Usmanov's Russian friends. If he failed to pay, Templeton might become a permanent cripple, or his children might suffer, or his beautiful wife might have acid thrown in her face. Subtlety was not his strong suit.

Templeton assured him he understood.

Usmanov walked into the bedroom he used for an office and pulled out a file marked "Templeton Private." He opened it and smiled at the prints of Templeton and his hot model wife. The small drone had done its work for nearly a year. Templeton and his beautiful wife slept with their window curtains open. They enjoyed looking out at the New York City skyline at night with the bedroom lights off. It also enabled Usmanov to use the small drone to take infrared videos of the couple having sex and walking around their penthouse in the buff. He even knew the size of the president-elect's member, which for some reason had been hotly debated in one of the primary debates. He couldn't quite understand Americans and their politics. But he knew their expensive lifestyle gave him enough videos and still photos to fill a bookshelf.

And his technicians had even synchronized the audio from the listening devices with the video taken by the drone. He shared copies with close associates and oligarchs who had financed Templeton. They were a hot commodity among his friends. He had heard they even showed them at parties.

It was always good to have a position he could leverage. Yet he had begun to doubt they would ever need any of it, which was all to the good.

He worried now that Templeton was president-elect the Secret Service would feel compelled to snoop around his condos. Just in case, copies of all of the secret files had been carried out of the building in a couple of thumb drives early this morning. The listening devices could be removed overnight if needed. They were ready to vacate everything at a moment's notice. He couldn't trust the Secret Service.

During the campaign Templeton had talked kindly of Russia. It was as if he had a sixth sense about these things. The guy was smart and crafty, he thought. As long as he kept playing nice, Usmanov might not need to consider blackmail.

For now.

He would meet with Platkin and others to carefully craft a blackmail strategy. They now had a puppet in the White House. They needed to decide how to pull the strings carefully. They must play them as skillfully as a violin, he thought. Templeton had no choice but to cooperate. He appeared to have gotten that message during the campaign whenever the subject of Russia came up. But one never knew what Americans would do, and especially Templeton. He was so unpredictable.

Yet how could he choose not to? What could Templeton say? Go public that he was in bed with Russian Premier Platkin? Ridiculous. What a place for Templeton to be in. Lose his empire or lose the presidency.

For now, they would wait. The listening devices were still in place. Knowing the president-elect's plans could prove invaluable. Pressuring him on other issues could come later. They would be patient. After all, Usmanov had just returned from a meeting in New Jersey with Domnin and the six oligarchs who had loaned Templeton more than half of his net worth. Two of the loans totaling nearly a billion dollars were coming due next year. And private auditors for the Kremlin estimated Templeton didn't have the cash flow to pay.

With Crofton now out of the picture, they had no obstacles blocking their path to a seat at the table with the next president of the United States.

Everything was in place.

XIV

Usmanov had just sat down for an American beer and to watch the late-night news when his doorbell rang. He clicked his remote, and his security system pulled up Domnin on his television monitor and standing at his front door. What did he want at this hour? Doesn't he ever sleep? They just spent hours together in New Jersey in strategy meetings. Enough already.

He opened the door, hesitated and then welcomed him in.

"Good news comrade," Domnin said.

"Don't comrade me here. You know better. This is the United States. You never know who's listening."

"Sorry. But I have good news. The technicians went through the videographer's entire file and found nothing, except video of us standing in the crowd at the Crofton party. No audio. They can't hear a thing we said."

"That is good news. Now go to bed. I'm beat."

"But don't you want to discuss?"

"Tomorrow, Domnin. Tomorrow."

Usmanov motioned him to the door and almost slammed it in Domnin's face as he turned around to say something. Usmanov didn't care at this hour. He knew he would hear early tomorrow from Domnin. He never shut up and he was staying right next door.

He went back to his television and flipped on the news. More about Templeton. These Americans were obsessed with politics, he thought.

When did they find time to talk to their neighbors or go shopping or visit the cinema or be irritated by the Domnins of the world?

He thought about what Domnin had said. He had Domnin watch the damned video twice before giving it to the tech to review. They had seen the girlfriend fumble with her microphone, but they didn't know what that meant. They worried her microphone might have picked up their brief exchange. That stupid Domnin. His loud mouth forced them to impersonate FBI agents and grab a copy of the video just to assure they hadn't been recorded. He knew Domnin was trouble the moment he set foot in America. Stupid oligarchs. They know how to make money but they don't know how to keep their mouths shut.

At least they needn't get rid of the photographer. He seemed amiable enough, but if he had recorded their conversation, he would have to be dealt with. Usmanov hated cleaning up others' loose ends. While it was sometimes necessary, it always made him sad. Those people had families and friends too. They did not deserve to die, but sometimes they were in the wrong place at the wrong time. Tragic collateral. That's how he thought of it. He sometimes wondered if his more ruthless colleagues had no feelings at all. Maybe they uncorked their emotions with their vodka late at night.

He took another sip of his drink and set the glass down. His eyes closed during a commercial after the weather forecast predicted a cloudy day tomorrow.

XV

Stacy Woodson looked at her watch. The president-elect was arriving in less than two hours. She and her team of Secret Service agents scoured Derrick Templeton's Florida estate in ritzy Palm Beach trying to secure it as best they could. Templeton had not visited the estate since he had received government protection back in February, preferring the confines of his New York penthouse and his Long Island mansion on the Sound.

No one ever dreamed the government needed to secure this property, which was why she was in charge. Most of the women in the Secret Service were relegated to the lesser candidates, the ones who weren't supposed to win. She was in charge of Templeton's protection now because Crofton had insisted the Secret Service place a woman in charge of her own detail.

That could soon make things awkward, Woodson thought. Right now, some of her staff in New York were still being debriefed about the assassination. Eventually, she would either take the fall for the assassination or would be allowed to move on. She figured her career would suffer no matter what.

But for now, she had a job to do. Templeton's Florida residence was similar to his New York penthouse. The top floor was filled with French faux glitter and gold. The historic mansion had more than one hundred rooms and was purchased from the heir to a pet food fortune. The grounds included seventeen luxury condominiums whose owners had rights to the complex, including use of the club restaurant, ballroom, and pool. That was a security problem, Stacy thought.

The estate had acquired the nickname "The Palace" because of Templeton's affinity for gold fixtures everywhere. Templeton, a man of simple tastes, apparently believed anything French was classy and sophisticated. When she had inquired about all the glitter, the Florida staff told Stacy that Templeton's idol was Louis XIV. She got it.

His Republican detractors ridiculed his taste as running the gamut from Cheese Whiz to cheeseburgers. Of course that view ignored his taste for expensive overcooked steaks. He may have fed his working-class supporters political red meat on the campaign trail, but he preferred his well done.

She stood in the ballroom taking in its grandiosity when one of her agents approached and handed her a list. "Here are the names of the condo owners."

Stacy stared at the sheet. Shit. Corporations owned thirteen of them. All shells, no doubt. They had no time to deal with that right now.

She turned to her agent. "Give this to the regional office and tell them we need a rundown of owners immediately and to give us whatever they have on each one. Tell the crew we're going native this weekend. Search everything, everybody. We'll get this place buttoned down eventually. Tell the Miami office to cancel all time off. We need everyone up here. We don't know what we don't know yet."

XVI

Tish felt like she was on an obstacle course. She had followed Grant's instructions to the letter and was finally walking into the bar in Park Slope in Brooklyn. She had been instructed to take two taxis and two subways to assure she wouldn't be followed. The guy was either super careful or super paranoid.

It hadn't been easy for Grant either, she figured. He told her Leigh Child didn't agree to meet with her until after a third phone call this morning. The woman, if nothing else, was stubborn. Or paranoid. Or both.

Tish stood just inside the door to let her eyes adjust to the dark. It appeared to be a typical Irish pub. What was with Grant and Irish pubs? A long bar stretched across one side of the room, tables in the middle and booths lining the opposite wall. There appeared to be a second dining room in the back and dark wood everywhere.

From the street, it looked like a hole in the wall, yet it was surprisingly large. She walked to the rear of the bar area as she had been instructed and slipped into a booth, making sure she faced the front door. She waited. Leigh Child would approach her. Grant was specific about that when he'd called late this morning.

She was grateful he called. He'd done as promised. So many sources she had dealt with in the past had made big promises and never delivered. She figured someone who had gotten as far as Grant had in the political world made a point of it.

Tish shed her coat and placed it on the bench beside her. She looked up and noticed an attractive blonde sitting alone at the bar drinking clear liquid on ice out of a twelve-ounce glass. Curious, she thought.

Just then, a waitress arrived and placed a glass of water and menu before her. It was the same size glass. Tish ordered white wine and kept her eyes on the blonde. Grant had described Leigh as a tall blonde. Would she signal her? She thought this was all a bit melodramatic. But Grant had made her promise not to approach Leigh at any cost.

The blonde turned toward Tish and glanced for a moment before pulling a cigarette out of her purse and turning back toward the bar. The bartender lit it for her. Smoking in restaurants and bars had been illegal for years in New York. As far as Tish knew, you could only smoke in designated cigar bars.

"Good afternoon," came a voice from behind her.

Tish was startled and looked up over her shoulder. Another tall blonde stepped in front of her and sat down across the table. She had a large purse she set beside her and no overcoat.

"Looking for me, I assume."

"Leigh?"

"Yes."

"Jim Grant's friend?"

"The only one. Nice to meet you, Tish. Jim told me you want to write a story."

"Yes, he said you could help."

"On one condition. Neither my name nor my method is ever used in any story you write."

"Then how do I legitimize my story?" Tish looked at the woman. Grant had described her as breathtakingly beautiful. He was certainly right about that. She was dressed in an expensive off-white silk charmeuse blouse, designer jeans, and a gorgeous black jacket. Tish couldn't fathom the price tag. Certainly above her pay grade. It was a posh, casual look a doctor could afford.

Tish felt way out of her league. But at least she wore her new designer jacket and blouse. Her outfit gave her a sense of confidence, although she felt overdressed in this pub. They both were.

"You write that our friend was examined by a doctor, and you obtained a copy of the doctor's unpublished notes and diagnosis. You can't say how you obtained a copy. That's the only way I cooperate."

Tish had no choice. If it wasn't enough for a story, she would just keep digging. "Okay. I can go along with that."

"Good."

The woman turned to her large beige purse and pulled out a blue loose-leaf notebook. "This is a copy of everything. My diagnosis is in front. All of the supporting material is in the back. I've also copied some journal articles on dementia to give you some background."

Tish couldn't help herself. She had to ask. "Why all of the caution?"

"First, this is a breach of my professional ethics and could cost me my career if it gets out I'm involved. And have you ever heard of the Goldwater Rule?"

Tish shook her head.

"Here's a journalism lesson for you, darlin'. Doctors can't publicly render a mental health opinion of a public official from afar due to their professional ethics. We lost our First Amendment rights to free speech when Senator Barry Goldwater sued and won a libel suit against a magazine when it published a survey of psychiatrists questioning his mental health following his 1964 presidential campaign. Now I don't know if that rule applies to me, since I actually spent time with Templeton, but I'm taking no chances. Just be aware you might get sued for printing this.

"And there's another reason I'm cautious. I spent several months with Templeton's campaign. I heard enough to scare me. He may be losing his mind, but he has some very scary friends. I agree with Jim Grant. He and the people around him present a real threat to the United States. That's the only reason I am breaking my ethical oath and talking to you."

"I appreciate what you're doing," Tish said.

"Tish, he is a dangerous man. His arrogance, I have no doubt, will likely get us into a lot of trouble throughout the world in the next four years. His ignorance will likely get a lot of people killed. His mental illness—and that's what it is—will draw power-crazed individuals like flies to swarm around him in hopes of taking advantage of his mental deficiencies. I don't know who he will surround himself with in the White House, but if it's the same people he had in the campaign, then we're in a lot of trouble."

"You're a therapist—"

"Psychiatrist. Big difference."

"Sorry. You're a doctor. Not a politician. How do you know so much?"

"I spent nearly three months within arm's length of the man. Not only is he mentally dangerous, he's a lech. I lost count of how many times he pawed at me. One time he grabbed my breast. I actually kneed him in the groin. The next day he acted like it never happened."

"You are very attractive." It was easy to understand why men were attracted to her, Tish thought.

"Thank you. I know how to fend for myself. He's one of the worst I've dealt with. From a medical perspective though, he is a fascinating subject. A pure narcissist. He was a joy to analyze, but he was a handful. Yet he can also be endearing at times. He was one of the most interesting evaluations I've ever done."

The waitress brought Leigh a glass of water with lemon and asked if she'd like something to drink. Ice tea was fine, Leigh said. Tish handed the waitress the menu and said they were just having drinks. That should get rid of her for a while, Tish thought.

"So are you going to take a job in the White House?"

"It's tempting. I'm talking with Templeton's people. Jim wants me there to keep an eye on things. I'm supposed to fly down to DC today and meet with the transition office sometime in the next few days.

"I understand where Jim is coming from. I'm not sure if I want to continue. I have a life. This is very disruptive. The problem is Jim knows me too well. He knows I'd jump on a case like this. Templeton is just so fascinating. I don't want to give him up. Cases like this are my weakness."

"That sounds fascinating. What else can you tell me about him?"

"That's enough. I think we're done. Please leave. I'll stay another five minutes after you've left."

Tish was put off by her abruptness. She didn't know how to react. She laid a twenty on the table figuring she could expense it, and she wanted to impress Leigh. She stood, pulled on her coat, and slid the notebook into her own purse.

"Thank you," she said, and began to walk away.

"You're welcome," she heard from behind her. Tish didn't look back but glanced over at the blonde smoking at the bar and pushed open the door. The bright November sun immediately blinded her. She turned and walked down the sidewalk in the direction of the subway.

LEIGH SAT STILL FACING THE WALL when Jim Grant stepped out from behind a partition that divided the bar from the dining room. He sat across the table from her.

"How'd it go?" he asked.

"Fine. She'll do. She seems so young though."

"I know. I had to make do. After Crofton's death, I was operating on the fly. Things happened so quickly. You think I made the right move?"

"I don't know. I guess we just wait and see," Leigh said. She looked at him and frowned. "You might have just put that young girl's life in danger. You okay with that?"

"Do we have a choice?"

"I think I'm going to work in the White House. I think I'm safer under his nose than going home and suddenly disappearing on some dark road one night."

"You really think some of Templeton's people are involved?"

"It's just a gut feeling. He's not stupid, and he always has a steady stream of—how should I phrase this?—interesting people coming through his office."

Grant looked up toward the bar and then back at Leigh. "She's leaving."

"Good. I think I could use a cigarette too, and I don't even smoke."

They laughed. Grant watched the blonde as she stood up at the bar and walked over to open the heavy wooden door to the street. Leigh turned to look. Grant didn't know the blonde's background. But Leigh had done her homework. She'd hired an experienced bodyguard who packed a pistol under her skirt and another in her purse. What gave her away, but usually went unnoticed, was the shoes. Flats. She never wore heels. Leigh chose well.

"It's time for us to leave too," he said. "Mustn't linger. Your babysitter is waiting."

"I don't know if I'm cut out for this," Leigh said.

"You're doing great. You're doing the right thing. Trust me."

XVII

Tish found a near-empty car on the subway with only a few elderly men sitting at the other end. She began flipping through the notebook and found an initial report and several articles about dementia copied from different academic journals. A clear plastic sleeve in the back held a thumb drive labeled "Old Interviews."

When she stepped into Tom's apartment she quickly realized he wasn't there. No note. Nothing. Well, she guessed he really didn't owe her one. It wasn't like they were living together—well, at least not for more than a few days.

She slipped the drive into her computer and began to watch old television video clips of interviews of Templeton from ten and twenty years ago. After about ten minutes, the screen was split in two, showing a young Templeton on one side and Templeton from the fall campaign on the other. He was asked the same question by two different interviewers on each half of the screen. The younger Templeton was articulate and gave concise and detailed answers. The older Templeton stumbled over words and constantly repeated the same phrases.

Grant and Child were right. The video made it clear Templeton was losing a step. Why had no one else noticed? When that idiot woman had run for vice president years ago, everyone including the media jumped on her case. But not a man. They gave a man a pass. Well, she wasn't going to do that.

She called Meryl at the office to tell her what she'd found.

"Write me something. A quick outline with the facts, and I'll get back to you in an hour," her boss said.

Tish typed up a quick two-page summary without any sourcing and emailed it. During her orientation period, Meryl had taken her out to lunch and explained how Washington was chock-full of anonymous sources. Some more important than others. But they were never to be referred to in email. The paper also destroyed all email after ninety days. So anonymous source material needed to be kept offline and somewhere only the reporter could find it. The paper was extremely concerned about government electronic snooping. It had become all too easy in the internet and cell phone era.

An hour later, Tish still had not heard back and was tempted to call. But she knew Meryl, and she would be in touch when she was ready. Another hour passed, and then her cell rang.

"I've got good news and bad news for you," Meryl said.

Oh great, thought Tish. They want her back in Washington right when she's on the trail of something.

"The bad news is I'm losing you. The good news is you're being promoted to the National Desk," Meryl said. "You impressed enough people down here, and they're short a reporter. So I put your name in. Nancy Moore is going to be your new editor."

"Isn't she the special projects editor?"

"Something like that. She used to be city editor but now she is tied to the National Desk. This is great for your career. Just about all of the big stories go through Nancy. Her nickname is Holy Shit, although obviously we don't ever use that around her. You'll hear her use the four-letter word frequently and Baker loves Holy Shit stories. Those are the ones—"

"I know," Tish interrupted, "the ones when readers say 'holy shit' after reading them."

"I've got to be honest with you," Meryl continued. "You did most of this on your own. Baker was so upset with our national team over its Crofton assassination coverage he decided to pull you up. You impressed the right people down here. Your memo on Templeton's mental health didn't hurt you one bit."

Baker was Executive Editor Robert E. Lee Baker, the warhorse of the newsroom. When he cracked a whip, the place jumped. He had turned a mediocre newspaper into a great one. He got everything he asked for. You did not tell Baker no.

"Oh."

"Oh? Is that all you can say? You just got promoted to the National Desk. You're now officially on the President-Elect Templeton beat for one of the best newspapers in America. If I were you, I'd go out tonight and celebrate. But not too much. We want you on the beat bright and early tomorrow morning. Tell that boyfriend of yours to take you out someplace special this evening."

Tish couldn't believe what she was hearing. She hadn't been with the newspaper a year and she was already promoted to cover the next president of the United States.

"I don't know what to say. I'm—I'm—"

"Shocked? Flabbergasted? First thing you say is 'thank you Meryl.'"

"Thank you—"

"Oh stop. You don't need to thank me. But it was nice of you to think of it. Tish, you did it yourself. I just hate giving up this new story you're working on, but it's better to give it to Nancy. She's got the background and resources. Hang on. I'm going to transfer you to her. Good luck now."

She was placed on hold. She waited. And waited. Finally she heard a click on the phone.

"Where'd you get this?"

"Hello?"

"Tish, it's Nancy Moore. Who's your source?"

Welcome to the National Desk, Tish thought. Could she catch her breath first? She'd just learned—.

"Source?"

"Sorry. I'm a little taken by surprise about the change in my status."

"Yeah, well, it won't last long if you don't give me your source."

Tish explained the story, the videos, the notes, and meeting both Leigh Child and Jim Grant over the past two days.

"And Grant fully acknowledges he's got a bone to pick with Templeton?"

"He seems on the up and up to me."

"And what about identifying the doc?"

"She won't have it. Strictly background. Not even a description. She fears for her career as well as her safety."

"The career, I get," said Nancy.

"That's the other side of this story. There seems to be some undercurrent that things aren't completely kosher in the Templeton campaign."

Tish was sitting at Tom's kitchen table looking at the grimy walls and imagining the hustle and bustle of the *Post-Examiner* newsroom right now and how she was now a part of the big-girl club. But she was sitting here, alone, in a cheap apartment with thin walls begging for fresh paint and a kitchen hatched out of the seventies. Not exactly the debut she had imagined for herself on joining the National Desk. Reality, she thought, has a way of keeping one's ego in check—unless of course you're the president-elect of the United States.

"Honey, campaigns never are. But I haven't heard of anyone inside a campaign fearing for his or her own safety. Keep plugging on that one," Nancy instructed. "Write me a first draft of this mental health piece, and then we'll examine it together."

"Okay."

"By the way, you can call me Nancy, and welcome aboard." The phone went dead.

Tish could see things would be different on the National Desk. But she was excited at her assignment. Nothing had been said though about how much time she was to spend in New York. If she was covering Templeton, why wasn't she following him to Florida? She needed to figure this out quickly.

She spent the next two hours writing a story about what she had learned. It ran to more than three thousand words—a book in the newspaper world. No doubt her new editors would make their cuts and suggestions. She decided to sit on it for a half hour and then reread it. She wanted her first piece for her new editor to not only be a great story, but damned well written. She still had a lot to prove.

XVIII

Templeton entered the large dining room of his large private club. It was barely a quarter full. Sales at his Florida resort had been off during the campaign. He was counting on his presidency being good for business.

His lawyers on the ride down had told him he must sell his business interests to avoid any conflict of interest as president. He'd made it clear he spent a lifetime building his real estate and oil empire, and he wasn't about to sell. They had argued he had no choice and he had replied he sure did. He'd agreed to no longer take an active role in or salary from the business, but that was as far as he would go. He also agreed to give it to his sons to manage.

He would still own everything and take in his millions in profits each year. He'd figure out how to handle the conflict of interest later. He knew rules were made to be broken. He'd done it his entire career. Why change now?

He had also called his Florida club manager from the plane. "Double the initiation fee," he'd said. "I'm president-elect. They'll pay more now to see me."

HE AND MELINDA SAT at a table in the middle of his club dining room. She looked fabulous in her form-fitting designer outfit that showed off her voluptuous figure. He liked everyone in the room looking at him with envy.

Secret Service agents were at two adjacent tables and milling about the club.

"Derrick!" came a voice from across the room.

He looked up to see his old business associate Barry Winston. He stood, and the Secret Service agents took a step forward. Templeton waved them off and shook hands with his old friend.

"Really, Derrick. Metal detectors to enter the club?"

"I had no idea," Templeton said. He turned to look at the agent near him.

"Routine security, sir," the agent said.

Templeton turned back to his friend. "Yeah, well, I guess things have changed."

"I'd sure say so," Winston said. "And congratulations, by the way. I never—" He stopped.

Templeton leaned in. "I never did, either," he whispered. "I was running for four years from now. And look at me now."

They both laughed and patted each other on the shoulder, their ongoing handshake held firm in competitive recognition.

"Derrick, you're always ahead of the curve."

"Have to be to be a success in life. Winning is everything, you know."

They released hands, and Winston returned to his table. Templeton sat down knowing the Barry Winstons of the world—once his competitors and sometimes his business partners—would now want to pay homage to him. They would all want a political favor at some point and he would make sure he exacted a heavy price.

A well-done strip steak arrived. Kobe beef. His favorite. Melinda sat before her tiny Caesar's salad and glass of water splashed with lemon.

He sliced into his steak and looked up as he popped the first piece into his mouth. Across the room sat a solitary familiar figure. Templeton knew him as Demetri, but he wasn't sure that was his real name. But his money was real. That he knew.

Templeton owed him a fortune. He subtly nodded to Demetri, and the Russian businessman was just as subtle back. Templeton returned to his carving. Now that he was about to become president, he wondered what it would mean to his relationship with Demetri. His oldest son,

Aaron, would be handling the details of any new deals. He could no longer be involved.

The refinance was due in March, not much more than a month after his inauguration in January. He knew the deal had the potential to threaten his empire.

While he bragged publicly his holdings exceeded $10 billion, he never mentioned how much his assets were leveraged. In fact, he owed $7 billion in loans—mostly mortgages on his properties and oil wells. That made his net worth about $3 billion, but as long as his cash flow remained strong, he could make his payments and the public would never know the truth.

That still did not erase the need to refinance, and he faced a real problem there. He had structured some big notes that were now coming due. He needed to renegotiate some favorable terms to remain flush. He wondered if the presidency might hinder that process. Would Demetri try to leverage his position and force a tougher deal now that he would be president? If he were in Demetri's shoes, he certainly would.

Templeton had been extremely careful during the campaign to say nice things about Russia and to compliment that prick Platkin. Templeton didn't need to antagonize his biggest noteholders at this point or he could risk losing his business empire.

When he had first signed the note with Demetri and that Usmanov fellow five years ago, he thought he was dealing with dirty money. He never thought he'd have to pay it back. Hell, he'd done the same thing a couple of times before.

But his lawyer later told him this money had been laundered and cleaned up quite nicely. If he failed to make his payments, the banks the Russians fronted could seize his properties.

Templeton knew it was worse than that. The goons had also threatened to harm his family if he failed to pay. Of course, now they were all protected around the clock by the Secret Service. Let them try to get to him.

He needed to take advantage of his situation. After all, when you owe the bank as much as he did, you normally own the bank and can negotiate your own terms. Except in this case. He knew the bank he was dealing with was backed by an unlimited supply of Russian capital, so he had no leverage. He wondered if the Russian people understood how much a handful of oligarchs had stolen from them just to lend the future president of the United States their money.

He sliced through another piece of steak. God, he loved Kobe beef. This was from his personal stock flown in from Japan especially for him. He served his members here at the club the domestic stuff. It was cheaper and far more profitable.

He had to think of some way to deal with the Russians. Many of his loans were balloon notes, their full value coming due next year. He had borrowed the funds to escape the recession and bankruptcy. No one knew how close he was to losing it all, yet now he was on a roll. Real estate was hot again, even if his energy companies were not.

The Russian sat there staring at Templeton while Templeton examined him with passing glances. They were acknowledging their relationship. The Russian then folded his napkin on the table in an elaborate display, rose slowly from his table, assuring others in the room noted his presence, and walked casually out the door.

From now on, Templeton knew his relationship would be different. Arm's length at best. No more golf outings at one of his courses. No more indulging in late-night vodka parties with prostitutes while Melinda slept in the next room. This new job and his security detail would surely get in the way. He wasn't sure he liked that part of becoming president. But as the next leader of the free world, he figured he could do anything he wanted—just like he had done his whole life. Like any other business problem, he would find a way to fix it.

XIX

Tom arrived at the apartment a few hours later and explained he had met with a cable executive wooing him for a job. They were impressed with his election night footage.

"You didn't tell me." Tish felt hurt. Wasn't this the type of stuff couples talked about first?

"Oh. I'm not interested in the job. I just was testing my market value to see if I should be charging clients more."

"And?"

"About what I'm making now. And besides, my upside of working alone is much better. I only need a few catastrophes like election night to clean up."

She felt relieved. It was nothing serious. She realized she struggled with insecurities about their relationship, yet Tom gave her no reason to.

"Tom, we need to talk about the audio track you're keeping from the FBI." She watched him, and he immediately braced himself. "What is it? What bothers you about them?"

"Nothing."

"Tom. We agreed no secrets between us."

He looked at her, obviously irritated.

"What did the FBI say to you when I wasn't here that got you so uptight about your audio track?" she asked.

"They asked accusatory questions that made me feel like I'd done something illegal. I mean I get it. I was standing right next to the damned weapon that killed Crofton. But another photographer stood on the other side too. Thirty guys were on the platform, and no one thought much of it. I didn't put it there. So why are they focusing on me?"

"I don't know, hon, but I'll bet they would be a lot happier with you if you gave them the audio track."

"I'm thinking just the opposite. I'd get accused of withholding evidence, and they would be even more suspicious. I don't trust these guys. I don't like their pressure tactics. You're just going to have to trust me on this one. I may change my mind later depending on the circumstances, but right now I'm hanging onto it, if for no other reason than protection."

"You're talking like someone who is guilty."

"Is that what you think?" Tom visibly bristled at her suggestion, his eyes aflame with anger.

"Of course not. Tom, you know how I feel about you."

"I'm sorry. This whole thing has me confused and angry."

"It's turned both of our lives upside down. Tom, I'm sorry." She could feel her eyes glisten. She grasped his hands in hers.

"Let's get back to some semblance of normal," Tom said.

He looked into her eyes and gently took her hand and led her to the bedroom. He slowly peeled off her clothes and she did the same to him, fumbling with his belt buckle and lowering his boxers. She grasped the obstacle in her way, gently squeezing it, and his boxers finally reached the floor.

She desperately pulled his face to hers and kissed him hard on the lips.

Suddenly, he picked her up by her bottom, and she wrapped her legs around his waist and he lowered her onto him. God, he felt good, she thought. He rocked her up and down and soon quickened his pace. Her breasts felt momentarily weightless with each rhythm as he held her aloft.

She had no idea Tom was so strong. He pumped more. And again. And then she felt him explode, and it felt good to please him. But he did not quit. His rhythm continued as he rocked her world in pleasure until, yes, yes, she gasped and gripped him tighter with her thighs, and she felt it too.

He slowly lowered her to the bed and lay down beside her, kissing her nipples and stroking her breasts. Her body rippled with excitement. Then he raised his head, and they kissed, their tongues locked in an embrace that caressed her soul.

For the next hour all thoughts of assassinations, cameras and politicians were erased from her mind. Nothing could invade their world.

XX

She had been expecting the call from Washington. Holly Crofton's death had happened on her watch, and now she was going to take the fall. Stacy could feel it coming as she sat in the window seat in economy class descending into Reagan National Airport. The glare of the early morning sun thwarted her efforts to spot landmarks she had come to know over the years along the Maryland side of the Potomac River.

By the time she arrived at FBI Headquarters on Pennsylvania Avenue, Stacy had prepared for the worst, so she was surprised at the greeting she received.

"Special Agent Joel Kopperud," said the only agent in the entire building courageous enough to wear a brown suit. The FBI hierarchy tended to like its clones. Even she wore her navy-blue chalk-stripe uniform to this meeting.

He shut the conference room door behind him. "I'm not here to give you grief. If there's any to be had, that will come from your own folks over in Treasury. I want to bring you up to speed on the Crofton investigation. You impressed me during the debrief the other day, and I thought it best for us to try to work together. I hate the way the departments compete. We need to work as quickly as possible on this, and I need your help to do that."

"You've got it," Stacy replied. She remembered him now. He was among the five agents who had interviewed her for nearly six hours the morning after Crofton's murder. But he was the one sitting alone, behind everyone else, and he hadn't asked a single question. He'd listened and she saw him jot down the occasional note. It was like he was analyzing every word while the others talked over each other and her.

That's why she hadn't remembered him immediately. The other four, she could pick them out of a lineup any day. Boy, she didn't want that experience again.

"First, I want to show you some street camera footage." Kopperud flipped a switch, and a street scene of downtown New York City appeared on the wall monitor at the end of the long conference table. He immediately froze the image and took out a laser pointer from his pocket.

"Here's the guy. Right here. Coming out of the subway station. Note the two satchels. Notice the shapes. One is for the weapon made to look like a camera, and the other is for the tripod. Smart of them to use the subway. Makes it harder for us to follow a trail."

She looked at the photo. A slender man, maybe in his thirties, wore a baseball cap and sunglasses to hide his face. The mustache and goatee were obvious fakes.

"We're enhancing the face. Should have a good facsimile later today."

He started the video and immediately flipped to another camera angle.

"This is footage from the hotel lobby. You can see him walk in and head toward the ballroom. Now this—" He stopped to fiddle with his computer. "Here you see him leaving nine minutes later. This was around four in the afternoon. No one was in the ballroom except for a janitor or two, some technicians setting up on stage and a couple of security guards at the doors. No Secret Service yet. Your people didn't sweep the room until five. By then, crews had probably set up half a dozen cameras. Unfortunately, the hotel has no security cameras in the ballroom."

Kopperud doffed his jacket, dropping it in the chair beside him and returned to the computer. He punched a few more keys on a laptop.

"Now look here." He again swirled his laser pointer at the screen. "This street scene was taken by the camera just outside the hotel at five o'clock. Note the panel truck pulling up across the street. Curious thing. If you watch it long enough, which we did, no one ever gets out of the truck. So we figured they operated the remote camera weapon from here."

He tapped a couple of more keys. Same camera on the truck. Different time. It was dark, but the truck was directly under a streetlight. Not the best spot if you wanted to remain inconspicuous, but this was New York. It was a parking space.

"Now check the time stamp. It's twelve twenty-two. One minute after Crofton is shot. Watch." He tapped a key, and the video began. Blue exhaust blasted out of the tailpipe. The van backed up a few feet, and then the wheels turned into the street and the truck drove away.

"That's no coincidence. That's our killer. We checked the license plates. They were stolen. We found the truck abandoned in New Jersey late yesterday afternoon. Forensics is all over it, but so far, nothing. I'm sure the killer wore rubber gloves. So far, all we've found is dog hairs that belonged to the owner's pet. The owner said he didn't even know the truck was stolen. His story checks out. It was taken from his company's parking lot. It's normally used to make deliveries for an auto parts store that had closed for Election Day. The owner is an active Democrat who works the polls on Election Day. Says he has closed on Election Day for the past thirteen years. We're trying to narrow down who knew that, but it's like finding a needle."

He didn't finish the phrase. Stacy understood.

"What about the weapon?" she asked.

"We stripped it down or at least what was left of it. It appears their plan was to completely destroy it. The firing mechanism not only sent a bullet into Crofton's brain, but also ignited a small explosive to destroy the weapon—the evidence. Instead, it sparked and fizzled and didn't do a whole lot of damage. I mean the device will never work again, but it left us a lot of forensic evidence. That appears to be our best lead, and we're still working it.

"All we know is, the operator of the weapon could see everything through the camera inside the machine. It served as a remote gun sight. It's similar to those miniature video cameras they place on small drones—the ones you buy your kid for Christmas. The rest of the fake camera body housed the weapon itself. So the operator could literally zoom right up with crosshairs on Crofton's head and know he had the shot. He couldn't miss."

"It looks like you have the entire setup figured out," Stacy said.

"We do. We just don't know who yet. Everybody slips up. This guy had to slip up. And it doesn't look like a single assailant did it. It was too well-timed. I figure the scheme included a driver and an operator in the truck."

"Why's that?" Stacy asked.

"A hunch. The setup guy left the hotel the same way he arrived, through the subway. Now he could have had the panel truck parked somewhere nearby, but we would have picked that up on our street cameras. So far, nothing. We're expanding our search. I'm sure we will eventually figure out from which direction he came. But also, after the shooting, we clocked only seconds between the time Crofton was shot and the van pulling away. Someone operating a remote would have been sitting in the back, closed off from the front seat where anyone could see him. The truck has a sliding panel between the seats up front and the back where spare parts are usually carried. The camera operator could do his job in complete secrecy."

"What can I do to help?"

"Like I said, we have no footage of the ballroom hours before the shooting. We've confiscated copies of all the footage from the camera-men who were in the back of the room. Some pretty gruesome stuff, but nothing enlightening. We were hoping some of your guys who were on the scene might remember something. I'd like you to take this informa-tion I gave you back to your team and see if it might spur a memory of something from your crew."

"Happy to." Stacy felt good. Two elite government teams were actu-ally working together. And she was not on the chopping block yet. But it had to come. That was the way the government worked. If only she could somehow help solve this mystery, maybe she could save her job. Then she realized what was going on. Kopperud was trying to do just that—trying to save her job. Why was he being so nice to her? She didn't even know him.

And then the conversation turned dark and she began to understand why she was really summoned to Washington.

XXI

Tish was on the phone to the FBI Public Affairs Office in New York, seeking the latest information about the investigation. She was told to contact the Washington headquarters. She did, and they hadn't released anything new. So she called Secret Service Public Affairs and was promptly referred to the FBI. She loathed the government runaround.

Public Affairs personnel were supposed to help reporters and the public by releasing government information. What she always found was just the opposite. They were nothing more than guardians at the gate to assure the government released as little information as possible. And this was supposed to be an open government of the people. Sometimes it just made her shake her head.

Finally, she called the New York Police Department.

"Nothing new," said a young woman over the phone. "But you might want to join us for a news conference in two hours. I think you'll learn something there."

A sense of urgency emanated from the woman's voice. Tish decided to take her advice.

ABOUT THIRTY REPORTERS were waiting in the conference room for the chief of police to show up. Someone who identified himself as a public information officer was blathering on about the speakers.

Not another one of these people, thought Tish. Just let us hear the chief.

Finally, after a lengthy introduction filled with platitudes, Chief Timothy Donaldson stepped to the podium.

"Good morning," he said. "At one forty-five this morning, the assassin of Holly Crofton was captured without resistance in an apartment in the Bronx."

The chief slowly waded through a prepared statement, as if he were struggling with a first-grade reader. He should take speech lessons, Tish thought.

"He was transported to headquarters where he is currently being questioned. I'll take your questions now."

"Who is he?" shouted a reporter from the back of the pack.

"Right now we're not giving out his identification."

"How did you find him?" yelled another.

"Good police work."

"Did he act alone?" Tish shouted.

"Right now, we're not sure. We believe her assassination involved more than one person. It was well organized and appears to have been the work of at least two individuals, if not more."

Twenty hands flew into the air, and just as many questions were shouted in unison.

Donaldson raised both hands to calm the pack. "Settle down, folks. I'll try to get to all of your questions, but before I do, I'd like to show you some video."

He nodded, the lights dimmed, and traffic camera video of a subway entrance appeared on a large monitor behind him. Donaldson pointed out their suspect, who was carrying two satchels.

"As you can see, he's carrying the weapon and a tripod in separate cases," he said. "He walked into the ballroom and set up his weapon and left."

The chief then showed another traffic camera video and pointed to a panel truck parked outside the hotel.

"We believed the remote camera was operated from this vehicle parked outside, across the street from the hotel."

When he was done, hands flew, and several reporters began shouting again.

"Do you have any video of the suspect inside the hotel?" asked a reporter.

"Only in the front lobby," the chief said. "Unfortunately, the hotel did not have any security cameras in the ballroom."

Tish realized that was why the FBI, and even the fake FBI, were after copies of Tom's video and probably all of the other cameramen's work, as well.

It was slowly beginning to make sense.

XXII

Stacy thought their conversation was wrapping up. She had been talking to Kopperud for nearly an hour in this windowless room. The door was closed and it had started to grow uncomfortably warm.

She had thought the FBI could do better, what with the scratched furniture and nicked walls. But it had spent its funds on upgrading its technology and not on conference room tables and chairs in the aging, broad-shouldered bunker known as the J. Edgar Hoover Building.

"What I just told you is for public consumption," Kopperud said. "It's what everyone believes right now—the FBI, the New York police. Right now, the police chief in New York is holding a press conference releasing this information. It's the official version. It's what they want the public to believe. I'd say forget it, except it's the story you need to relay to your agents. If you don't, the higher ups here will know about it immediately and both of us will be toast."

"I don't understand." Stacy looked at him curiously. What was he talking about?

"I think it's all bullshit. I think I've figured out what really happened."

He spent the next ten minutes taking the conversation in another direction.

"But there's nothing I can do," Stacy said. "I'm on thin ice as it is. Is that why you confided in me?"

"I saw what was happening in the Bureau. They think my explanation is a crock. They were determined to quickly close the case—to find some-one, anyone, to take the fall for Crofton's murder. It's all cover-your-ass around here. Everyone is trying to pin the blame elsewhere for Crofton's murder while nobody's doing their job to track down the real culprit. They'll be coming after you soon. I need someone who is personally motivated to get to the truth. Nobody fits that bill better than you."

"But I'm damaged goods. If I go out there and tell the world the FBI screwed up, it will mean my career for sure."

"But don't you see? If you could somehow explain how the FBI botched the investigation, maybe we could save your ass."

"Joel, that's very sweet of you to try to help me. But I'm a big girl. I can handle myself. I've been with the Service for fifteen years. I know its office politics. I know how it works. This would not help me one bit. What might help is if you can release that information and make it public some other way. Through some disinterested third party. This thing needs to crumble on its own legs. Anything traced back to me would have no cred."

"Who then?" he asked.

"The only one I can think of off the top of my head is that reporter for the *Post-Examiner*, the one who was killing the competition on election night. She's got a couple of things going for her. She's young and hungry, and she's not jaded by all of the corruption yet. She's new, so our file on her is thin. We got the call just yesterday from the *Post-Examiner* seeking a White House press pass for her. Looks like she's going to be around for a while dogging Templeton."

"You really think giving this information to a reporter is the right way to go?"

"Right now, it's the only way. It adds credibility. And because of her inexperience, you can probably spoon-feed her any information you want. You can mold this. You know what I mean? This is your opportunity to get the exact story you want out there. When she gets more experience under her belt, it might not be so easy."

THE FBI AGENT'S TEASE WAS enough to get Tish on the next Acela train to Washington. He had explained he'd liked her recent work and wanted to talk to her about the man the New York police had arrested. He explained they must meet somewhere in private and she'd suggested a restaurant a block from her new apartment.

When she stepped in the front door, she encountered a new neighbor she had met last week. The woman, who appeared to be leaving, asked if Tish would like to grab a quick drink. Tish explained she was meeting a friend. She also realized she'd just made a rookie mistake. She needed to hold a meeting in a place where neither she nor her source would run into anyone they knew.

Lesson learned.

Kopperud had given her a description, and he was easy to spot. He had his back against the wall in a booth near the rear of the room. Duh. Right out of the movies.

"Joel?"

He nodded and she sat down across from him. He had short blond hair and green eyes. He was slender and wiry and looked very intense. But still, he was rather good-looking.

"Friend?" he nodded toward the front door.

An FBI agent, she reminded herself. He didn't miss much. "Yeah. I made a mistake. I should have found a place where I didn't know anybody. But this is quiet and private otherwise."

"The New York police arrested the wrong man for Crofton's killing," he said softly.

"What?" Tish couldn't believe what she was hearing.

"They're desperate to save face—both the FBI and the New York police—mainly because they don't have any other suspects right now."

"I wondered why they never identified him."

"Exactly. They didn't even arraign him. The FBI talked to the judge, who is allowing them to hold the man indefinitely. But indefinite is not forever. It's not like he is some enemy combatant or something."

"Who is he?"

"I don't know. I'm not privy to that part of the investigation. They are staying pretty closed-mouth."

"Then how do you know he's the wrong guy?"

"The evidence is bullshit. That part I do know. That's my area of expertise. My people have been examining the weapon. Our part of the investigation has gone better than we had hoped. The weapon had a self-destruct mechanism that didn't work properly, so we have more of the weapon intact than the assassin had planned on.

"The video the police chief showed you this morning was based on the assumption the weapon was operated remotely from the van outside. But we picked up no identifiable frequencies in the street that could communicate with the camera."

"I don't understand."

"Let's just say we are able to pick up all of the chatter, all of the radio frequencies when we are around the president or presidential candidates. Will you trust me on that?"

"I guess I have to. So what does this all mean?" For someone who was twenty-four years old, Tish knew she should be more technologically savvy. She was good with her cell phone and little else.

"Like I said, the self-destruct mechanism on the weapon failed. It destroyed only a portion of the camera. So we assumed part of the weapon that was destroyed was the antenna that would pick up a frequency from its operator outside the building. It was on that assumption that the police arrested their suspect." Kopperud looked up and surveyed the room.

"But?" Tish persisted. She didn't care who was there. They were sitting far enough away from anyone else in the nearly empty restaurant. She was sure no one could hear them. But she wasn't the FBI. She wasn't paranoid like this Kopperud fellow.

"We've been meticulously taking the weapon apart over the past few days, and then yesterday we discovered a Bluetooth connection. It was partially destroyed, but it was wired into the operating system of the weapon."

"Meaning?"

"The operator of the weapon that killed Holly Crofton was not outside in a van, but inside the ballroom using the hotel Wi-Fi the entire time."

"Oh my God," Tish almost screamed and immediately placed her hand over her mouth. Kopperud looked past her out at the empty room. Tish turned around to look. A couple of kids were getting frisky at a booth near the front door, and three office workers were having beers at the bar. The bartender had a towel over his shoulder and one in his hand drying glasses. No one looked their way. "Sorry. I didn't mean to make a scene."

"We're okay."

"Why are you telling me this?"

"I need your help. The New York police and some here in the Bureau refuse to acknowledge they don't have the assassin. All they've got is his accomplice. They are under pressure to wrap this up in a pretty bow and be done with it. Meanwhile, the real assassin is still out there."

"The man in custody didn't pull the trigger?" Tish asked.

"Exactly. He couldn't have."

"But what about the van outside? What was the person doing in there?"

"That took a while for me to figure out. And then it seemed so obvious. We suspect whoever fired the weapon remotely from inside the ballroom, also immediately called or texted the van and signaled the deed was done. Had something gone haywire, and the weapon not gone off, whoever was in the van was there to pick it up after the party. That way they would be leaving no evidence behind, and no one would suspect there had even been a plot to kill Crofton."

"So someone with a cell phone standing somewhere in the ballroom set it off?"

"Possibly. I think more likely the shooter had to have been using a tablet computer of some kind connected by Bluetooth technology to the weapon. They still had to aim the thing, so they would have been staring at a bull's-eye on a screen while everyone in the room was screaming and partying on the ballroom floor. They would have been pretty conspicuous."

"So who then? Who fired the gun that killed Crofton?" she asked.

"One of the cameramen in the back of the room, I suspect. They were the only people who could be staring at a screen during the bedlam of the moment, and no one would pay them a bit of attention.

"Someone staring at a cell phone in the crowd while Crofton was entering the ballroom would have drawn the immediate attention of the Secret Service. Agents were lined up along the front of the stage surveying the crowd. None of the team recalls seeing anyone doing that. They are specially trained to notice suspicious behaviors. But the agents paid no extra attention to the cameramen."

"Don't the camera crews need press credentials to get in?" Tish asked. She knew she did.

"Yeah. The man who delivered the weapon showed the guard at the door his credentials from one of those foreign press syndicates. We checked with the syndicate the next day. No one's ever heard of the guy," Kopperud said, shaking his head.

"So do you have a new suspect?"

"That's where it gets awkward. You see, the number one suspect right now is your boyfriend."

Tish felt faint and sick to her stomach. Now she understood why Tom wouldn't cooperate with the FBI.

XXIII

As soon as she exited the restaurant, Tish called Tom. He did not answer. She left him a message to call her. She didn't want to say any more. She took a cab straight to Union Station, not bothering to go by her new apartment a block away to grab some clean clothes. She jumped on the first train to New York and called him three more times. He never answered and she never left a message.

Where was he? All of her insecurities about their relationship began to bubble up. She needed to bury those feelings. She set her laptop on one of the tables in the café car and began to write her story. She led with the New York police having arrested an accomplice who couldn't possibly be Crofton's assassin. The real assassin was someone unknown in the ballroom. She left out the part about all the cameramen being suspects, including Tom. She knew she was probably wrong in doing so, but she couldn't bring herself to write it. Besides, she had no proof, she told herself, only Kopperud's supposition.

She knew it couldn't be Tom. She just knew it.

She emailed her piece to the National Desk using her cell phone's hot spot. The Amtrak Wi-Fi was too slow. She almost sent it to Meryl on the City Desk by mistake. It just seemed so natural. She hadn't gotten used to the idea she had moved up in the pecking order of journalism. Thirty minutes later, her cell rang. It was Nancy Moore. Tish walked Moore through the details and sourcing of her story, watching her words as people walked by ordering sandwiches, soft drinks, and the occasional beer. Nancy was satisfied.

"You've done it again, girlie," Nancy said. "I think this will look nice on the front page tomorrow morning."

IT WAS EVENING BEFORE she walked through the door of Tom's apartment. He wasn't there, but he'd left a note on the kitchen table.

"Call this number as soon as you get home," he had written. She read the local number and dialed.

"Police," came a woman's voice.

"I was given this number to call by my boyfriend, Tom O'Neal. Is he there?"

"One moment."

She was placed on hold. She looked around the apartment. Everything seemed fine. Nothing was disturbed, nothing missing—.

There, she saw it, or rather didn't. Tom's camera equipment bags were gone. He usually kept them in the corner of the living room next to a bookcase.

She searched the apartment, cell phone to her ear, just to make sure. She was looking in the bedroom closet when she heard a click on her phone. "Ms. Woodward, this is Sergeant John Fielding. We are questioning your friend Tom and have a few questions for you as well. Mind coming down to the precinct and talking with us?"

"Will I see Tom?"

"Yes ma'am. Not a problem." He gave her directions, and she was out the door.

THE PRECINCT WAS TYPICAL New York shabby. While the politicians all pledged to be tough on crime, that didn't mean they'd actually appropriate money to stop it. The precinct showed signs of their indifference. The design on the linoleum floor tiles had worn off leaving a path to the front desk. And Tish guessed some of the furnishings were older than she was. The walls were scratched, dirty and showed signs where graffiti had been scrubbed clean. Some disgruntled people who didn't want to be here had defiantly left their mark.

The desk officer, looking as bored as a tollbooth operator, directed her to wait and someone would be with her shortly. Unlike her phone call, this time she wasn't placed on hold for long. A young officer appeared in less than a minute and escorted her through narrow halls to a dull green interview room. There sat Tom at a dented metal table, looking exhausted.

She entered, and the officer closed the door behind her, leaving them alone. They embraced. Tom let out a large sigh. That opened the floodgates for Tish. They stood holding each other for more than a minute. Then Tish pushed back and wiped away her tears and his.

"What's happened?" she asked.

"They're accusing me of somehow firing that weapon and killing Holly Crofton."

"That's absurd. How can they say such a thing?"

"They confiscated my equipment. They say my camera's Bluetooth connection was used to fire the weapon. I know other photographers who use Bluetooth. I like it because if I have a good Wi-Fi connection, I can upload raw footage for later editing or send it immediately to a client. I'm sure my hookup is different from others' since I wired it myself. I don't have a network tech. Mine's jury-rigged, which makes these cops suspicious."

Tish heard the door click behind her and turned around. The young officer was there.

"Ms. Woodward, Sergeant Fielding wants to speak with you," he said.

She turned to Tom and looked into his eyes.

"Alone," the officer said.

She embraced Tom and turned to follow the officer through the door. He led her to a room at the far end of the hall, which was identical to the one Tom was in.

Fielding arrived and instructed her to watch Tom's video again. So, for the umpteenth time she watched herself fumble with the microphone. It appeared obvious she was not familiar with the equipment, but the officer seemed to imply otherwise.

"I find your attitude offensive," she finally said. "My boyfriend and I have done everything within our power to cooperate. I don't understand why you can't accept that on face value."

"It's our job to look into every possibility."

"Am I a suspect?"

"No, ma'am, you're not. You're an eyewitness. That's all this is."

"Is my boyfriend a suspect?"

"At the moment, no. But we ask that you both not leave town," he said in that bored, 'Why am I here?' voice cops often use.

"That's impossible. I'm a reporter covering the president-elect. I may have to fly to Florida. And you can't keep me from leaving town."

"You're right about that. But we know where to find you. Today in DC, tomorrow morning New York, or any day, anywhere."

That sounded like a threat. How did he know she was in Washington today? Had she been followed when she met with Kopperud?

"Unlike your department, I have nothing to hide," she said, anger oozing from every pore. She had had enough.

"Are we free to leave?" she asked Fielding.

"One moment." He stood and left the room, closing the door behind him.

This did not make sense. The police were suddenly pursuing other suspects after claiming they had the suspect in custody. Kopperud told her they had refused to look further. What happened between her meeting with him earlier today and this evening? Maybe they got a whiff of today's meeting with Kopperud. Maybe that's what this was all about.

Ten minutes later, Fielding returned. "You are free to go. You'll find Mr. O'Neal out front in the waiting area."

She walked through the hallways back toward the entrance to the building and spotted Tom with his camera and two satchels of equipment piled in an empty chair in the front waiting area. She was eager to leave. It was late, after eleven, and she was tired. She grabbed the lighter canvas bag from him. It was his tripod. The police had returned it.

Tom wrapped his free arm around her shoulder and held her tight as they walked through the double doors to the street.

And then it dawned on her. Sergeant Fielding had probably already read tomorrow's story online. That's how he knew she was in DC today. She'd given her story a Washington dateline. Maybe she wasn't followed after all. And that might also be the reason why she and Tom were allowed to leave. The police didn't need more egg on their face by retaining the reporter who wrote a critical piece—a story that was absolutely true. Better to be rid of them, she thought, than risk angering her and giving her something else to write about.

She felt a sense of her own power as a journalist and it felt good.

But why had they suddenly changed direction and started pursuing other suspects?

As they hailed a cab, Tom explained the police had come to the apartment in the early afternoon and insisted he accompany them, along with all of the camera equipment he'd used on election night. They had allowed him to leave a note for her but not to make a call.

Tish was flabbergasted. She wondered if that was legal.

"Don't they need a warrant or something?" she asked, remembering the Russian agents who took their video without one.

"I don't know."

Maybe she wasn't that big of a threat after all. She needed to make sure she didn't get careless or too full of herself.

XXIV

In the taxi, Tish told Tom about her story in tomorrow's paper. All the cameramen were now under suspicion, not just Tom. When they reached the apartment, Tom suggested they share a bottle of Scotch he had been given last Thanksgiving, more than a year ago. "I'm not much of a Scotch drinker. I haven't even opened the bottle. But tonight, I think we need something strong," he said.

Tish was happy to join him on the couch even though her favorite poison was a nice dry red. The drink was potent and she felt her head quickly gravitate into a light buzz. Then Tom reached over and kissed her. His breath tasted like hers, and together that made it all right.

After they emptied their glasses, they stumbled to the bedroom together. Tom fell on the bed, and Tish went to the bathroom. When she returned, he was asleep—again. It had been an awful day for both of them, but especially for Tom. At least they were together.

He could never have done what they had accused him of. Could he? Her suspicious nature bothered her. She knew it was good for her job, but she needed to leave the job outside Tom's apartment. Inside, she told herself, should be their sanctuary from the madness that had engulfed their lives in the past several days.

Oh, she was kidding herself. Both she and Tom had been doing most of their work from here. He thrived here. They had no sanctuary from all of it except in each other's arms. Thank God for brief moments like tonight.

She slipped into bed and wrapped her arm around his hairy chest. She kissed the back of his neck and closed her eyes.

XXV

It always took Tish two cups of coffee before she could realize she was vertical in the morning. She sat at Tom's kitchen table and reread her story online twice before she could focus. Her editors had done a nice job.

She glanced at the bedroom door, behind which Tom was still sleeping. She wondered if she could survive this without him. It was like someone had flipped a switch, and their lives had shifted into overdrive. It was intense, and it was what she had always wanted. Yet she never dreamed how stressful the ride would be. She needed Tom to help her balance her perspective on the world right now.

She couldn't imagine him guilty of anything. But even the thought made her anxious about their relationship. Could she really be in love with him if she had any doubts? The idea bothered the hell out of her and she thought it said more about her than him. Maybe she just wasn't ready for this. For him. Maybe she was kidding herself about what he meant to her. One thing was sure—she needed to get a grip. Her job was beginning to consume her life.

She heard the soft ding announcing a text on her cell phone. The message said "Urgent" and from the National Desk.

"This looks like it's all your fault. Nice work," wrote Nancy. "The FBI and New York Police Department are holding a joint press conference at ten. Be there."

Tish headed for the shower. It was show time again and she wasn't about to miss this one.

Suddenly, she was wide-awake. Adrenalin, it turned out, was a much better drug than caffeine.

XXVI

Even Tish felt embarrassed for the FBI and New York Police Department. They set a new record for groveling, acknowledging their suspect was not the assassin.

Police Chief Donaldson justified the arrest noting the man they had in custody was an accomplice. And he still refused to release the suspect's name. That showed a lot of confidence.

Tish could hear the snickering among the news media and felt the room's collective eyes on her even though she was sitting in the back. It was the first time she felt other media people were conscious of who she was.

"Does this mean Crofton's opponent, Senator Steve Berry, is no longer a suspect?" asked a reporter.

"He never was," said Donaldson. "I don't know where you got your information, but he was never under investigation."

"Was the *Post-Examiner* story accurate?" ask a reporter from the *Associated Press.*

"As far as it goes," he said.

"Meaning?"

"The news media are famous for getting only half of the story. The other half of the story is that we are now looking into every cameraman who was in the ballroom. You should ask Ms. Woodward how she feels about cameramen."

Everyone turned around and looked at Tish. She felt her face flush with anger. She bit her lip. She was sure they were extracting what revenge they could. It was another reminder she was playing big-league ball.

Almost by instinct she flung her hand in the air and spoke without being called upon. "Chief, is it your position that you can't attack the veracity of the *Post-Examiner* story, so you're attacking its writer instead?"

Donaldson paused and then stuttered. "Well, uh, well, no, uh—"

"So you're acknowledging the accuracy of the *Post-Examiner* story?"

"That's not what I said."

"But that's what you mean, isn't it?"

"No."

"Then what's wrong with the story?"

The reporters were all looking at her. She noticed grins on many of their faces.

"Well, nothing, I guess." The chief looked from side to side to his aides, seeking rescue.

They stood silent.

"You guess?" she shot back.

"We found nothing wrong with the story. There. Satisfied?" The chief appeared to actually be pouting.

"Thank you for clearing that up," Tish said. "Now what are your problems with the journalist who wrote that story?"

"I didn't say I had any problem."

The room roared with questions. She had just put the man in charge of New York's Finest in his place. She just showed the room of big league reporters she belonged. And she hoped she had steered attention away from her boyfriend. She was now glad he had not revealed the existence of the separate audio track. She too no longer trusted the authorities.

Ten minutes later, after another round of tough questions, the chief left the stage. He'd had enough. Half a dozen reporters came up to Tish.

"Nice questioning of the old man. I haven't seen him squirm like that in years," said the *Associated Press* reporter.

"Just be forewarned," said a *New York Journal* writer. "You have just made an enemy for life. He holds a grudge and he'll be gunning for you."

She decided it best to leave before someone asked about her relationship with a certain cameraman.

XXVII

Nancy Moore was impressed. The new kid had done a decent job on the story about the president's mental health. It wasn't complete, but it was amazing and damning.

She asked the research staff to run a check on Leigh Child. She was the real deal. Had been in practice for fifteen years. They even found some articles she had written for several professional journals.

Nancy also ran a check with the political staff on Jim Grant. He'd been a political operative for a long time. Worked his way up in the Democratic Party and had been in communications in several high-profile election campaigns.

Everything checked out. She kept trying to justify the story. Everything it included was solid. But she was uncomfortable with the anonymous sourcing. The paper certainly used its share of anonymous sources, but this was too big a story to be based totally on an unnamed informant. They needed someone on the record. This was, after all, the future leader of the free world.

She picked up the phone, called Tish, and gave her the bad news.

"Sorry. Keep digging. We need more," she said.

TISH WAS STYMIED. She hadn't gotten any real direction from the National Desk. She was in New York while Templeton and most of the national media were in Florida and her editors were in Washington. She felt like the kid on the sidelines looking at the field through the chain link fence while everyone else was playing the game. And yet, she was the one hitting the homeruns. How could that be?

She called Grant and explained her dilemma. He was not pleased.

"What can I do?" she asked. "I need to somehow verify all of this with an on-the-record source. They just won't go with anonymous sources on something this huge."

"She's the only one who has been close enough to examine him," Grant said. "Wait . . . what about his personal physician?"

"Really? You think he'd release private medical records? I don't think so." That came out too sarcastic, she thought. She needed to tone it down, especially since Grant was a friendly.

"But what if I could get ahold of those records?" Grant asked.

"I assume you're talking about doing something illegal."

"I didn't say that."

"I can't base a story on stolen property."

"I'm not talking about stealing anything. I'm talking about his life insurance policies." Grant's voice changed. Tish heard an air of confidence.

"What do you mean? Why would someone that rich need life insurance?" she asked.

"You are a babe in the woods. It's called estate planning. Sure, he's got numerous corporations and partnerships, but he also has lots of investments and cash on hand. Should he croak tomorrow, if he did no estate planning, he'd give it all to Uncle Sam, or at least a huge chunk. So, the rich, they buy various forms of life insurance to save their estates from the IRS. To do that, they must give the insurance company their medical records or have a new medical exam. I've got to think his physician has something on his diminished medical state."

"Just how do you get a copy of his life insurance policy with medical records attached?" Tish asked.

"Leave that to me. I have friends."

"But you'd be stealing personal information."

"I promise, I won't steal anything. I have an idea. I think I can make them give it to me."

"And no false pretenses?" she insisted.

"You're a real Girl Scout, gosh darn it."

She didn't appreciate his sarcasm.

"No deception whatsoever," he said. "Look, let me make a few calls."

He hung up.

She had no reason to be leery of Grant. He had played it straight with her. Yet he still made her uncomfortable. Perhaps it was because he lived in a world that was anathema to her own. Yet neither could live without the other.

Go figure.

XXVIII

Grant was blowing smoke with Tish. That had always been part of his job description. But there had to be a way to disclose Templeton's mental status in some legal way that would make this *Post-Examiner* reporter comfortable enough to print it.

He had been suspicious for some time about Templeton's past and his Russian friends. The campaign's opposition research on Templeton before he had joined the national ticket showed some shadowy connections. Grant knew they had invested in some of Templeton's major properties. And before the Russians had arrived, Templeton had tried to secure cash in every way imaginable and had miraculously escaped bankruptcy.

He remembered talking to a big Wall Street campaign donor, Eliot Proxer, after a New York fundraiser Templeton had arranged for the ticket. It was obvious Proxer did not like Templeton. Grant had asked him if their vice-presidential candidate had any vulnerabilities he should be aware of, and the reluctant donor had said plenty.

Grant found Proxer's phone number and called.

"Grant here. You and I both have our doubts about Templeton," he began.

"Doesn't everybody," said Proxer. "He's a loon."

"When we talked last summer, you mentioned he had many vulnerabilities. We're trying to find them to know what we are dealing with. I've heard he may have some mental issues, but I can't verify that." Grant heard laughter over the phone. He waited. Proxer continued. Grant pulled the phone away from his ear.

"Sorry. Sorry, man. It's just so damned hilarious."

"If it weren't so serious," Grant said.

"Really? So, you finally figured out a man with the vocabulary of a twelve-year-old may have some mental deficiencies? Where the hell you been boy?"

Grant ignored the insult. "As you can imagine, this is sensitive. No one ever expected him to be where he is today." Grant was desperate. He needed something substantive he could take back to Tish.

"At least you got that part right."

"I need your help. I need to find documented proof. If necessary, it could be used to remove him from office. He is a dangerous man."

"We can certainly agree on that. You need proof, huh? That shouldn't be so difficult."

Grant listened. And waited. Silence rumbled loudly in his ear. He worried Proxer was reconsidering.

"Look," Proxer said, "it was, it was, well, seven years ago Templeton filed for bankruptcy for a number of his businesses. Now each is a separate corporation, so while that might raise a few eyebrows, no one really thought he was vulnerable. But the truth is, he desperately wanted to save one business because it was primarily his own money, and not investors who would lose out if it failed. He needed a cash infusion and finally found a lender in a state bank out in Colorado where his development was. Lucky for him, they didn't know him. You won't find anyone in New York City who will loan the son-of-bitch a dime these days."

"So what happened?"

"They made the loan contingent on him buying a life insurance policy as collateral. We're talking two hundred million dollars here."

"Okay, so?"

"Nobody gets a life insurance policy at that level without a complete medical exam. The policy is usually filed with the deed. But some idiot in the insurance company attached the medical exam to the policy, and another idiot—a paralegal from Templeton's own law firm—filed the whole thing in court for the whole world to see. After they realized their mistake, they tried to get the judge to remove it from the public record, but he refused.

"Once filed, it became part of the state legal records system. It's there, right on the computer in some local district courthouse in Colorado Springs. Jesus. What are the odds? What a screw-up. But lucky for you, right?"

"Who knows about this?" Grant was bursting out of his skin.

"Templeton's people, obviously. His attorney told me many years ago when I was still on speaking terms with that double-crossing bastard. I'd guess a dozen people might know. All it takes is someone to look. I mean he's a land developer for the most part. There are lots of things hiding in plain sight if you know where to look for them. I shit you not, my friend. No one has bothered to go find it."

XXIX

The flight to Colorado Springs with a layover in Denver had been smooth. It was a cold November afternoon, the sky was clear and the sun brilliant when Tish stepped out of the terminal and hailed a cab. Grant had called her the night before and she had managed to book the middle seat on an early morning flight.

She went straight to the courthouse and found the clerk's office. She sat at the computer terminal and began her search. Tish had no idea the name of the financial institution nor the name under which Templeton had borrowed the funds. And it had been around seven years ago. Geez, she was in high school way back then auditioning for a bit part in the class play.

She first looked up Templeton's name. Nothing. It made sense he wouldn't file something under his own name. She had no idea how to find the company.

She pulled out her cell phone and dialed the National Desk.

"Excuse me, ma'am," came a voice from behind her.

"No phone calls in here. You'll have to take that outside."

Tish got up and walked out into the hallway.

"Nancy," she said, "who is compiling Templeton's holdings for our files?"

"That would be Jacobson. He's our resident nerd."

"I need to talk with him. I need to find out what Templeton owns in Colorado."

"Hang tight. I'll find out and be right back." Nancy placed her on hold.

Tish watched the grizzled lawyers and what must have been young paralegals no older than her walking up and down the hallway. She could tell by their dress what their roles must be—tailored suits walking next to ill-fitting blazers and wrinkled kakis. It reminded her of Meryl's remarks about her own attire. She could see what Meryl was saying. It really did make a difference. She would thank Meryl the next time she saw her.

One of each entered the clerk's office while Tish stood there waiting. She paced and found the ladies' room. She entered and found a stall. When she was done, she walked back into the hallway. Still no Nancy.

She found a drinking fountain and took a sip. She walked to the front door and looked out into the blazing late afternoon November sky.

Finally.

"Grayson Tower," Nancy said.

"Thanks a million. I gotta run."

"Not so fast," Nancy interjected. "That's the name of the office building. It's owned by the Franklin Plaza Corporation."

"Is that another of his properties?"

"You want me to do all of your research for you? I just gave you enough info to find the Rock of Gibraltar. Geez, you're making me worry about you. You know what state you're in?"

Tish felt sheepish when she hung up. She admired Nancy's kick-ass style, but she'd yet to grow accustomed to it.

Tish reentered the clerk's office determined to unearth a treasure-trove of documents only to be immediately stymied. All of the computer terminals were occupied. The lawyer and the paralegal she'd seen enter earlier were seated before the last two, one of them sat at the terminal she previously occupied.

Damn it. She knew she needed to be patient. But she was concerned the clerk would close the office for the day before she could complete her research. Calm down, she told herself.

Finally, an elderly woman appeared to be logging off her terminal. The woman stood hesitantly in a blue shapeless shift, momentarily looking around until she found her wooden cane.

Tish locked her focus on the empty terminal. The outside world no longer existed. But the woman did not move. She stood there, blocking the machine. She appeared confused. Then suddenly, she walked unsteadily toward the clerk's desk, a dozen or so printouts in her free hand.

Tish logged in and waited. And waited. Finally, a familiar page she had been visiting before her phone call to Nancy popped up on the screen. She again had her bearings. She took a deep breath.

This time she typed "Franklin" into the search box. A page of Franklins slowly began to fill the screen. Government computers, she thought, always the slowest. She scanned down the page looking for Plaza.

Bingo. She clicked and there it was. A deed of trust for $200 million with the name Franklin Plaza appeared. And there in the third line was Grayson Tower. It was all here. Wow. She couldn't fathom so much money.

She scrolled down through dozens of pages of the legal document. Finally, she came to an attached life insurance policy. She scrolled more, looking for a doctor's exam of some kind. She stopped. She was looking at a list of results for dozens of medical tests for Derrick Templeton. She couldn't make out what any of the numbers meant, but was pretty sure she was looking at a blood workup. She pressed Print on the page and three more pages of tests spit out of the machine. Then she began to read.

The physician's diagnosis said Templeton showed signs of early dementia.

"It appears more severe than normal memory loss due to aging," his physician wrote. She read on. No mention of Alzheimer's. But, the doctor wrote, Templeton had cognitive impairment. "His memory was not always clear when examined and his vocabulary has declined significantly—now at the equivalent of an average sixteen-year-old male."

Tish stopped trying to comprehend what she was reading. This was the future president of the United States. She struggled to understand the implications.

Later, she told herself. Move on.

"When interviewed and asked a series of questions, the patient sometimes has difficulty answering in complete cognitive sentences," the physician wrote. It went on to use a lot of medical terms, none of which she understood.

She began printing everything. After she finished with the medical records, she printed the life insurance policy and then the deed of trust. In all, at a dollar a page, she was making the local clerk's office very happy. She counted her pages—seventy-three. She double-checked to assure she hadn't missed any, then stapled them together and logged off the computer.

After paying for her copies she grabbed a cab and headed back to the airport. On her way, she called Nancy.

"I've got it. Can we run it tomorrow? I can photograph it with my phone and email it to you."

"Hold on, girlie. Not so fast," said Nancy. "I want Hedelt in legal to look this over. Plan on spending tomorrow with the lawyer. And we need to get someone with a medical degree to read the test results. There could be a good story about the other medical tests as well."

She hadn't thought of that.

"That means I need to fly to DC instead of back to New York."

"Well, duh."

"See you in the morning."

XXX

Tish called Tom before her flight to tell him she was flying to DC. It would be her first chance in days to pick up some clean clothes, but she'd sleep alone for the foreseeable future. She spent the short flight to Denver and her layover in the airport reading over the documents and taking notes. She pulled out her laptop and wrote her story on the longer leg of her trip to Washington. It was dark outside her window and almost everyone else on the plane was asleep.

TISH ARRIVED IN THE newsroom at ten, the time she and Nancy had agreed to meet. It had allowed her to get a few hours of sleep after her long flight.

Nancy immediately took the documents and made two copies—one for her and one for Robey Hedelt, the newspaper's staff attorney. Before they started, she faxed the doctor's report to a physician often consulted by the newspaper's medical writer.

Nancy and Tish spent an hour going through the documents, skipping the legal language and descriptions in the deed of trust, except to assure Templeton's signature was on the document. Then they inspected the life insurance policy. Yep, it matched the deed of trust—$200 million payable to the lender should Templeton die.

Finally, they read the physician's notes. Nancy picked up the phone and got the doctor on speaker.

"Michael Palmer, meet Tish Woodward. She's the one responsible for this week's headache."

"Nice work, Ms. Woodward," Palmer said.

Tish thanked him and asked what it all meant. Nancy gave her a stern look. Oops. She'd just stepped on Nancy's lead. This was Nancy's show now.

"The material you have here clearly shows he was in the early stages of dementia. Just how severe that might be would need to be determined at a later date."

"Like now?" Nancy asked.

"Since this was seven years ago, I'd say there is reason to be concerned. He should be tested today by a specialist in geriatric psychiatry."

"I didn't know there was such a thing," Nancy said.

"There's a specialty for almost everything today," Palmer replied.

"You're ready to go on the record with your interpretation?" she asked.

"Sure Nancy, but understand, I'm reading another physician's records. I didn't examine him. But I can certainly interpret his diagnosis."

"Perfect," she said.

They spent the next half hour going through the report, even getting his analysis of the other tests. Templeton had high blood pressure, high cholesterol and the beginnings of type 2 diabetes. He suffered occasional impotence.

"Can you use that?" Tish asked.

"Everything but the impotence," Nancy said. "Let's give the man his dignity. His inability to get it up might even please his wife. God if I were married to him . . ." Her voice trailed off and she shook her head. "Let's put the other medical results in a sidebar. I want the main story to stick to the mental capacity issues. I also want you to find those old television interviews of Templeton you have and do a side-by-side with his most recent television appearances. See if you can visually see the difference. Have the geeks help you with that. We can post it online."

Nancy thanked Palmer for his analysis.

"Anything for you old gal. You will clean up my quotes before publication?" he asked, sounding concerned.

"Absolutely," said Nancy. "I'll personally polish your syntax. Need to approve?"

"No thanks. I trust you."

They hung up.

Nancy turned to Tish. "One hour. I want the additions in your story in one hour. I'll grab Hedelt, and we'll sit down and go over everything to make sure we're not sitting on some legal fault line."

Tish sat at her desk, which was still near the City Desk and Meryl, her editor the last time she was in the newsroom.

Ten minutes into her cut and paste and insertion efforts, her desk phone rang.

"Grant here," came the voice over the phone. "Any luck?"

"Pay dirt," Tish responded.

"I think I can make your story even hotter," Grant said. "I'm in DC. I came down yesterday to do some political snooping and job hunting. I scored a hit on the first and struck out on the second."

"I just got word some senators are investigating the possibility of creating a special committee to examine Templeton's mental state with an eye toward removing him as soon as he is sworn in."

"Who told you that?"

"The Senate Judiciary Committee's chief of staff. He's all over it. It's all very, very preliminary."

"Holy Jesus."

"Exactly."

"Will he talk?"

"Are you kidding? Not on the record," Grant said.

"Background?"

"He said as long as he wasn't tied to the story. I'll set it up if you like. I know he doesn't want you calling the office." He hung up.

Tish slowly placed the phone down in its cradle. If this was true, it could make her story even more powerful by tying Templeton's health to his removal from office. That could be dynamite. She had to tell Nancy. She stood to walk over to Nancy's desk across the newsroom, and then thought better of it. She would first find out if the committee chief of staff really had the goods.

Twenty minutes later, her phone rang again. David Morrell identified himself and told her he would talk on background—she could use his information as long as she didn't disclose him as her source. She agreed.

The Judiciary Committee, he said, was chomping at the bit to investigate the future president. Chairman Eugene Hollins, a Republican from North Carolina, did not like Templeton. He had screwed his brother-in-law out of a real estate partnership years ago. And even though the two had hung out in some of the same power circles around New York, his brother hadn't talked to Templeton in years.

"Oh, and that part about Hollins is off the record," he said.

Tish hated it when sources did that, when they declared something off the record after they'd already disclosed it.

He also explained the process under the Twenty-Fifth Amendment. It was not the same as impeachment, which was for high crimes and misdemeanors. If Templeton were removed, it would be for his inability to continue in office.

"What makes members of the Senate suspicious of Templeton's mental condition?" she asked.

"Off the record?"

"I'd prefer on the record."

"Sorry. That ain't gonna happen."

"Background?"

"Nope."

Morrell wouldn't budge. Tish realized she had no choice if she wanted a better understanding of what the senators were doing. "Okay then. Off the record."

"Numerous Wall Streeters have started complaining to members of Congress about Templeton's past. It started out with them moaning about how Templeton always screwed his partners in business deals, but then they started complaining about Templeton's behavior in recent years. Apparently, some of his behavior has gotten bizarre."

"Like what?"

"Sorry. I've given you enough."

After she hung up, Tish wondered why such an innocuous accusation had to be off the record. She figured it must be too easily traceable back to Morrell. Oh, the games she had to play to get the truth out to the public.

She changed her lead paragraph to reflect the Congressional committee angle. "The Senate Judiciary Committee," she wrote, "is investigating the possibility that President-Elect Derrick Templeton is mentally unfit for office, according to a source familiar with the committee's inner workings."

Her next paragraph was even more devastating. "The *Post-Examiner* has learned from court documents that Templeton's personal physician had expressed concern about the president-elect's diminished mental condition seven years ago. His doctor's prognosis was accidently made public as part of a life insurance policy purchased to back a real estate deal in Colorado."

Just then she remembered she hadn't contacted Templeton's doctor for a comment. She looked him up online and made the call. She explained to the secretary what she had and she was assured the doctor would return the call.

Nancy strolled by her desk. "Ready?"

Tish nodded and printed three hard copies of her story. She walked over to the printer and then followed Nancy into one of the many glass-walled conference rooms along the edge of the newsroom. She was introduced to Robey Hedelt. Tish had assumed their attorney to be a man, not an African-American woman like herself. She hadn't noticed many minority faces in the newsroom.

Robey stared. Their eyes locked for a long time, and Tish grew uncomfortable. Was she sizing her up? Was it her light skin? Tish had always lived in a world somewhere between black and white America, with both sides often showing their disapproval. But then Robey flashed a warm grin and her words of approval about her story helped Tish unwind some of her intensity.

They spent an hour going through her story. Nancy made several changes to clarify the writing and Robey gave her approval. When they were done Robey left for the corporate offices on the seventh floor.

Nancy handed Tish her marked-up copy. "I want it cleaned up in twenty so I can give it to the desk editors and Baker to read. And don't forget Templeton's physician's comments."

Tish walked to her desk and began. It was all nitpicking for the most part, but Nancy did shuffle some sentences around and flipped some phrases. She had to admit it was a smoother read.

She leaned back in her chair and looked at her desk. Except for a legal pad she'd been keeping notes on, it was spotless. The back of her neck felt the strain. It felt like she had been leaning over that damned laptop for days. She had lost track of how much checking and double-checking she had done on the story. And the desk hadn't even had a chance to make its edits.

She surveyed the newsroom. It was around five o'clock and the place was buzzing with approaching deadlines. She loved the energy in the room. She glanced at the City Desk. Meryl was talking to a reporter about her copy. She swung her view over to Nancy who was on the phone at the National Desk. Everyone seemed to be racing toward deadline. But not her. She was . . .

Shit. She hadn't head back from Templeton's physician. She had no hopes of him responding to her questions, but she needed to at least get a "no comment." She had even left a notation in her copy where to insert it.

She called him again.

Again, she was assured the doctor would call her back. She said she would hold.

"It's your nickel," said the receptionist.

She was right. It was her nickel. Or at least her employer's. Two of her colleagues were talking about a murder in Shaw a few desks away. Tish laid the receiver of her office phone on her desk and walked over.

"Can I ask you two a favor?" She explained her situation and they gladly agreed to help.

Soon, both were on their phones explaining they were from the *Post-Examiner* and wanted to talk to Templeton's doctor. They too were placed on hold. Tish pulled her cell from her purse and called the doctor's office. The line was busy. They had succeeded in tying up every phone line.

It didn't take long.

"Okay, you win," said the receptionist. "You've made it impossible for the doctor's patients to call."

"I just want to confirm something," Tish said. "I just need a little cooperation."

When he finally came on the line, the doctor refused to talk about the medical file. Doctor-client privilege, he said. That's all she needed and hung up. After giving her colleagues a high five, she inserted his "no comment" statement in her story and pressed send. It was complete.

Tish checked with Nancy.

"Go home. I'll call if I have any issues. You've done enough damage for the day." Nancy smiled. Tish hadn't seen her do that before.

On her walk home to her apartment, she called Tom.

"I've been going over the videos again. I found something interesting." He said he was going to try and catch the six o'clock train to DC.

That would put him here late evening, she thought. "I'm really tired. I'm going to take a nap. Wake me when you arrive."

"No worries sweetie. Love you." He hung up.

That was the first time he had ever said he loved her over the phone. She felt good. This had been a good day. She knew she'd sleep well.

XXXI

But she didn't. Excitement about her story—the most important of her career—kept her on edge. She was up when Tom arrived and he finally went to bed without her.

It was nearly midnight before the online version was posted. She read her new lead and slowly absorbed her entire story. She liked it.

The online crew's graphics and photos really enhanced the effect. She was thankful she now worked for a large newspaper that could quickly pull off such a feat.

The package included two separate videos of interviews with Templeton that took place a decade apart. To demonstrate his diminishing vocabulary, they placed Leigh's videos side by side of Templeton answering the same question years apart. The effect of time was devastating.

She couldn't have been happier. Finally, she lay down beside Tom, ready for bed, but she was still too excited to sleep. After a half hour of staring at the ceiling, she got up and poured herself a glass of merlot. At first, she sipped it. Then she guzzled. If she wanted to get any sleep at all, she needed to finish her wine. It worked.

She wobbled back to the bedroom and tumbled into bed. She fell so hard she woke Tom, who rolled over, acknowledged her reentry, and rolled back.

SHE AWOKE BY SIX, a bit groggy and with a headache. Then she realized what day it was and sat up in bed making her head hurt even more. Gosh she was a cheap date.

She grabbed her glasses and staggered into her living room, quickly realizing she was naked and returned to the bedroom to find one of Tom's T-shirts. One of the joys of being with Tom was wearing his T-shirts. They were large and comfortable and carried his faint scent. And they were long enough to cover all her essential assets.

She immediately turned on the television, which was already set for CNN. It was an advertisement. Of course. She walked into the kitchen and made a pot of her favorite coffee. She had just pressed the on switch when she heard the newscaster return.

"More on our top story. The Washington *Post-Examiner* reports the Senate is investigating whether to use their Constitutional powers under the Twenty-Fifth Amendment to oust President-Elect Templeton after he takes office due to diminished mental capacity. The newspaper cites medical examinations by Templeton's personal physician and an anonymous psychiatrist who both say the president-elect is mentally impaired."

The rest was just a blur. She walked back into the kitchen for coffee and then heard her name. "Woodward is the reporter who exposed the New York City Police Department for having detained the wrong man as the assassin of President-Elect Holly Crofton. Woodward has been with the *Post-Examiner* for less than a year and was thrust onto the national stage with her reporting on the assassination on election night."

Her cell phone rang. "Tish Woodward?"

"Yes."

"Tess Gerritsen, senior producer for *Morning Java* on MSNBC. We'd love you to swing by our studio and be on our show this morning. I know it's a last-minute ask, but you're the star of the day."

"I—I don't know," she said. "I would need to check with my editors."

"Would you check and get back to me?"

"Okay." She heard a click on the line.

Did she want to be on television? She thought about it for all of two seconds. Not this morning. She would discuss it with her editors later. She was flattered, but her fear of being exposed as unqualified for her new assignment was much greater. What would she talk about? She wasn't an expert on anything.

She needed to share this moment. She almost burst into her bedroom and then slowed down. She sat on Tom's side of the bed. He didn't leave her much room, but then she didn't need much. She gently shook his shoulder.

"Tom. Tom."

He rolled over. "Uh. Good morning. I guess."

"Tom, please get up. They're talking about my story on CNN. And MSNBC just called asking me to be on the *Morning Java* show."

"What?"

Tom was slowly joining the ranks of the living.

"You what? They did what?"

Well, maybe the ranks of the confused.

He pushed himself up on his elbows.

"Yes, they did."

"They did what?" he asked again.

"CNN talked about my story and even mentioned me, and MSNBC invited me to be on television this morning."

"Yo, girl." He turned and pulled his legs over to the side of the bed and stood up. He grabbed his boxers and looked for his T-shirt and then noticed it was on Tish. "Uh. I think you've got something of mine."

She slid over to the bureau and pulled out another T-shirt. He put it on, and she led him to the living room where CNN talking heads were pontificating in full-throttle mellifluous baritones. Not a feminine tenor or soprano among them, Tish noticed. Maybe she should be there.

They watched. When her story came on, Tom squeezed her shoulder. She absorbed his pride through his warm embrace.

After seeing the same story twice, they headed back to the bedroom to shower and dress. Their routine when they both were getting dressed was for her to take the first shower while he shaved because she needed extra time to put on her makeup and contacts. She was always jealous of Tom's twenty-twenty vision.

After she dressed, she went into the kitchen for a second cup of coffee and found the *Post-Examiner* on the counter. Tom had gone downstairs to retrieve her newspaper while she was in the shower. What a sweetheart. If he weren't in the middle of his own shower, she would kiss him.

There it was. Above the fold with a three-column, forty-eight-point headline. She glanced at it and stared at her byline. Finally, she turned to the jump page. There, she absorbed an entire page of photos, pull quotes, and excerpts from the legal documents. A side-by-side print version of the two broadcast interviews exposed Templeton's vanishing vocabulary. Wow, she thought. This is good.

Tom entered the room with a towel encircling his waist, and she flung her arms around him. "You are the sweetest." He hugged her back, and they kissed. Then he slipped his hand under her blouse and began to fondle her.

"Tom! It's seven in the morning."

"So?"

She smiled. "I love your dirty side."

They kissed again. She held him close, and she let his hands wander. She grew excited and wanted nothing more than to go back to bed. Then she pushed back. It was time to get serious.

She made him a full-on breakfast of eggs Benedict. When she wasn't paying attention, he sneaked a bottle of cold champagne from the fridge and opened it. He poured two glasses and turned in her direction. "A time to celebrate," he said.

As they sat at her table, Tom said his plans for the day were to go over to Capitol Hill and record some of the reaction to her story. "You?"

"I'm going to the office and figure out what to do next. Honestly, I haven't a clue."

WHEN SHE ARRIVED IN THE NEWSROOM, Nancy was hovering near her desk.

"Nice job. Baker wants to see you."

Baker? Executive Editor Bob Baker? She hadn't talked with him since the day he'd hired her.

She walked over to his office on the far side of the newsroom.

"Kid!" he said loud enough so the entire newsroom could hear. "Ya done good. Ya made us proud." He stood from his desk and walked over and threw his arm around her shoulder. "You just confirmed we made a great choice in bringing you on board. I'm looking forward to a long future here for you."

After some small talk, she thanked him and left. Her head was as light as helium.

"Okay, kiddo," said Nancy. "Party's over. Time for some follow-up. Get me some reaction from the Hill. McMurray will get the White House spin."

Templeton and his family had returned to New York for Holly Crofton's funeral at eleven. It was going to be broadcast live on cable news.

Tish sat down at her desk and powered up her computer. She started reading reaction from other news organizations. She was looking for some congressional reaction, but at eleven in the morning, nothing. Crofton's funeral was sucking all the oxygen out of the news cycle.

Finally, around noon, after it ended and President-Elect Templeton's motorcade delivered him to his New York penthouse, he tweeted. "Biased *Post-Examiner* once again proves it's fake news. Not going anywhere. Ask Congress. POTUS-elect healthy as an ox."

He wasn't about to allow Holly Crofton an unspoiled day of reverence.

The reference to Congress bothered her. She started looking online and found that a member of the Senate Judiciary Committee was denying any investigation was planned. Then another committee member from the opposing party chimed in and said the same.

Now she was beginning to worry. She looked up David Morrell's phone number. The committee staff director had given her his cell number earlier.

She did.

It took four rings before Morrell answered.

"What is this about the committee members denying they are looking into Templeton's mental health?"

"What do you mean? Of course they deny it," Morrell said.

"That's not what you told me yesterday."

"Yesterday? What are you talking about?"

"Yesterday you called me and told me the chairman hated the president-elect and was going to investigate his mental health."

"I did? I don't remember any such conversation. In fact, have we met? I don't seem to remember you."

Tish couldn't believe what she was hearing. "You called me yesterday."

"No. I don't think we've ever talked before."

"Then how did I get your cell phone number?"

"Half of Capitol Hill has this number."

"I can't believe you're doing this." She heard the click. He had hung up on her.

She walked over to Nancy, who was reading a story on her monitor. "We have a problem," Tish said. "David Morrell, chief of staff to the Senate Judiciary Committee, just denied our entire conversation took place yesterday."

Nancy paused and stood. "Shit," she said. "Welcome to Washington. This is what we call congressional ethics in this town. Sometimes you've got a story dead to rights, and they still deny it. He obviously got some serious blowback. So publicly he'll deny it. That's the problem with unnamed sources. They sometimes bite you in the ass."

"What do we do?"

"We need to prove we had it right, or they could make political mincemeat of your entire piece. You make one mistake, and they will try to discredit the entire story. I can see what's coming. If we can't prove we're right, we may be forced to run a clarification or maybe even a correction." Nancy bit her lip and shook her head.

Tish was stunned.

THE DENUNCIATIONS FROM the Democrats were swift. The president-elect went on a tweet storm. Even Committee Chairman Hollins, who she now knew hated Templeton, denied any such investigation was ever contemplated.

Tish called Grant. "What's going on?"

"They got spooked," he said. "Templeton's people unloaded on Chairman Hollins at six this morning. They threatened to delay nominating someone for vice president. Hollins hadn't considered that possibility. The longer Templeton can stall the nomination, the longer he can stay in the White House."

"But I thought it was Congress's job to nominate the new vice president," Tish said.

"It is. But in a practical political world, it's Templeton's choice. Otherwise, the Speaker of the House is next in line to become president. And Hollins hates him even more than Templeton. See what I mean?"

Tish was beginning to understand her dilemma. "Is there no way to prove the investigation was underway?"

"Not if the staff director is denying it. I always thought Morrell was a stand-up guy. Welcome to Washington, the town where the most courageous thing anyone ever does is run a red light."

"I just can't believe they tell me one thing one day and deny it the next."

"That's basic survival politics. And if you retract the story about the investigation, that will damage the credibility of the medical report. The public will conflate the two, and neither one will have any credibility." Grant paused. "Of course—"

"Of course what?" Tish interrupted.

"That's what this is all about," Grant said. "They can't deny the credibility of the medical report—Templeton really does have mental issues. So, they are denying the investigation exists in hopes of crushing the credibility of your entire story, including the medical portion. That's brilliant. I've got to give credit to someone in the Florida White House. They're not as dumb as I thought."

"What are you saying? This attacks my story and my credibility." Tish felt her stomach rumble and acid rise in her throat.

"But you have to admire the sheer audaciousness of those Templeton guys."

"I will never understand Washington's fixation with power," Tish said.

"Young lady, that's all Washington is," Grant said. "Listen, Tish, I owe you an apology. This is my fault. Had I not urged you to put this in your story, no one would be questioning the veracity of your story. I should have gotten a corroborating source."

"Lesson learned," Tish said. She hung up in disgust. How had things gone so wrong? She had been on one of the greatest highs of her life when she woke this morning only to see her day turn into rotted mush.

The television monitors hanging from the newsroom ceiling delivering the cable news stations were all carrying the same denunciations of the *Post-Examiner*. One congressional leader was even denouncing Tish. She wanted to bury her head under her desk and pretend it wasn't happening.

Nancy must have noticed her distress. Her editor was standing in front of her desk in seconds. "Let's take a walk."

Tish stood and followed Nancy. They stepped into one of the conference rooms. Baker quickly joined them. Just a few hours ago, he was congratulating her on a job well done. Now what?

"Bob, what do you think?" Nancy asked.

"Well, it's like this. We got our facts correct, didn't we?" They both turned to Tish.

"Yes," she said. "They're lying. My source, Jim Grant, says this is their only way of discrediting the medical report. The committee's chief of staff David Morrell denies even talking to me yesterday."

"I wonder why Hollins caved," Baker said.

"No doubt Templeton's people have something on him," Nancy replied.

"Grant told me Templeton is threatening to delay nominating a vice president once he is inaugurated. That's got them scared," Tish said.

"Someone on the Hill needs to read their Constitution," Baker said.

"You think we need to run something, Bob?"

Tish watched Baker mulling the idea of a story correction in his head. He tapped a small, unlit brown cigar on the conference room table and looked over at Tish again. "He called you yesterday, huh?"

"Yes, sir," she said.

"You call him back," Baker said. "You tell that little wimp if we hear one word that he is denying his conversation with you, that the *Post-Examiner* will file a slander suit against him and subpoena his phone records. That ought to shut him up. They want to play hardball. So will we."

"And what about a correction or clarification?" Nancy asked.

"Fuck'em. We stand by the story. We need to stand united on this one. They want to call us fake news? We'll call them what they are: gutless cowards led by a dangerously demented man who soon will be the most powerful human being on Earth. No, this is one we cannot afford to back down on."

Tish's heart surged.

"I'm going to go talk to the thumb suckers and finger pointers in editorial. They need to be on the right side of this one too." Baker turned back to Tish. "Kid, I hope you learned a lesson. You're in the big leagues now. They don't play fair, and they don't play nice. It's constant bloody warfare. You got your facts straight. You did your job well. That's how you protect yourself and this newspaper. Now go out and do it again."

Tish rose with a new sense of confidence. Just because she ran into a few bumps in the road, it didn't mean she hadn't done her job. Baker, with his experience, had seen the issue for what it was. That's all she needed, she told herself. More experience.

She went back to her desk and gleefully picked up her phone and called Morrell.

"David," she said. "The executive editor of the *Post-Examiner* just asked me to pass along a message. If we hear one word out of your mouth denying our story or your phone call to me yesterday, we will file a lawsuit against you and subpoena all of your phone records for the past month. Do you understand exactly what that means to your credibility?"

She was loving it. She didn't wait for a response. Instead, she slammed down the phone this time. It made such a loud noise she looked up to see if she had made a spectacle of herself. Nancy was again sitting at her desk and caught her eye and smiled.

She approved.

XXXII

Tish spent the rest of her day calling senators' offices for comment. Not a single press secretary returned her call. She suddenly was the Antichrist of Capitol Hill. The desk had decided to let McMurray write the follow-up story. It included a statement from Baker saying the newspaper stood fully behind the story. "We do not retract the truth," he was quoted as saying.

Tom called around four, saying he'd gotten plenty of footage for clients and had sent off several feeds already. He loved the press facilities in the Capitol.

"I didn't even know you had credentials," Tish said.

"Oh sure. Got them a few years back. I've know a lot of the guys down here for years, so it wasn't difficult to get a press pass."

She still had a lot to learn about her boyfriend.

"How about a pizza? Have one delivered to your apartment? I've got some video I want to show you."

She agreed. She'd forgotten he'd told her yesterday about wanting to show her something he'd found on his video. She ordered the pizza and told him she'd meet him at the apartment around five. She'd put in enough hours and anxiety for today. She checked in one last time with Nancy, who practically shooed her out the door.

"You've earned an evening off," she said.

TOM WAS SITTING in front of his laptop when she arrived home. He said he met the pizza delivery kid downstairs and brought the pizza up. It was in the box in the kitchen and still hot.

He rose, kissed her and ducked into the kitchen while Tish changed her clothes in the bedroom. She stripped and put on his T-shirt. She was happy to dump the bra and heels.

When she returned to the living room, she found pizza on the table, a bottle of red wine, and two half-filled glasses. Tom offered her a chair. She sat and then he sat across from her on her tiny dining room table she'd picked up at Goodwill for fifty dollars.

She told him about her day and how it had gone from joyous to disastrous and then back to happy land again. Tom tried to smile as he chomped down on some mushrooms. His side of the pizza was vegetarian; hers was pepperoni.

"You said you had some video to show me."

"I wanted to show you last night. But you were so wound up about your story, I thought it best to wait," he said. "And after your day today, I'm wondering if you're up for more."

"What is it?"

Tom wiped his hands and mouth with a paper napkin and moved his plate aside. He slid his laptop in front of him and started tapping the keys.

"You know the FBI said the man for Crofton's murder had to be inside the ballroom somewhere, right?"

"Yeah, and they said no one in the crowd that night could have done it except for one of the cameramen in the back of the room," Tish said.

"That was according to the Secret Service agents on stage, correct?"

"Uh-huh. They were watching the crowd, and no one was maneuvering an app on a cell phone or other mobile device that they could see. Everyone was just taking photos or videos of Crofton." She wondered where was he going with this.

He turned his laptop around so she could see the screen and tapped a button.

"The Secret Service was watching the crowd on the ballroom floor," he said, "not the stage behind them."

"What?" Tish watched the video. Tom had highlighted a man off to the far left of the stage next to several other men. Family and staff, Tish assumed, were gathered on the stage for Crofton's victory speech. The man was working his cell phone. Everyone else who was holding a cell phone near him was using it to record history as it unfolded.

"Oh my God," Tish said. "Do you think this man could be the shooter?"

"Who else could it be?"

"But why hasn't the FBI or Secret Service figured this out? They've seen this video."

"All I can think is they're focusing on the crowd to the exclusion of all else. Look at how they immediately suspected all the cameramen, including yours truly. Or how they claimed to have caught the assassin only for you to prove they had an accomplice in custody." Tom shook his head in disgust.

"Do you know who he is?" Tish pointed at the man.

"I have no idea."

"I know someone who can tell us."

XXXIII

Tom pulled a still of the person off the video and sent a file to Tish's computer while she was on the phone with Jim Grant. She emailed it to him while they talked.

"I know him," Grant said. "He used to work for Templeton. He was the most competent guy he had. Templeton insisted we put at least one of his people on Crofton's staff, so he was it."

"Who is he?"

"He worked in scheduling. Ended up as number three in the department only because they had no number four. But that's as good as Templeton's people got—a bunch of wannabe inexperienced campaign bozos."

"Yes, but who is he?"

"His name is Buckley Underwood, one of those rich Long Island preppy types. Family money. But despite his parents' best efforts to educate him in the best boarding school tradition, he was born without a brain, much like Derrick Templeton."

"Where do we find him?"

"He's in the Transition Office over on K Street. That's where all the people are who haven't been able to find a White House job," Grant said.

"Thanks."

"Wait a minute. You're not going to confront him, are you?"

Tish heard concern in his voice. "I sure am. He's the killer."

"Exactly. If he's killed once, I doubt he'd hesitate to do it again. Reporters aren't exactly popular in this town—with either party. You need some protection or reinforcements. Just how do you propose to do this? Make a citizen's arrest?"

"I haven't thought it through," Tish admitted. She examined the photo of Underwood while they talked. He didn't look so dangerous to her.

"Well, slow down, lady. Buckley ain't going nowhere. He'll be around in the morning. Their office opens at nine. I'd suggest you confront him there where he won't be able to do anything with his colleagues milling about."

"Good idea. Thanks for your help. And please keep this quiet," Tish urged.

"Don't worry. I want the SOB caught as much as you do. Take your time. Figure out how you're going to handle this."

She hung up and turned to Tom.

"His name is Buckley Underwood, and he worked in scheduling for the campaign. He now works in the White House transition office on K Street."

"What? Not smart enough to get a job in the White House?"

"I guess not. Jim Grant had a good question. How do we go about doing this? If we confront him, he's liable to run or something."

"First thing I'd do if I were you is call your editor," Tom said.

Tish felt dumb and pulled out her phone to call Nancy.

"You what? You're kidding," Nancy said. "How do you keep coming up with these monster stories? I'll get ahold of BB."

"BB?"

"Your boss, silly. Bob Baker. Let's plan on meeting at eight tomorrow morning in his office. I'll call you back if I can't arrange it."

XXXIV

Promptly at eight the following morning, Tish walked into the news-room. Nancy and Baker were already huddled in his office. Tish crossed the expansive room, weaving between desks, and sat in an empty chair left for her next to Nancy.

"Good morning young lady," Baker said. "Nancy tells me you've pulled another rabbit out of that hat of yours."

They talked about how to deal with Underwood. Baker suggested they have another reporter go with her. They then started going through names.

"Majors in sports," Baker said.

"What?" Nancy almost screamed. "He's a knuckle dragger."

"He's six foot three and all muscle," Baker shot back. "His presence will intimidate this Underwood character enough that he won't do harm to my star reporter." Baker looked right at Tish. His look of satisfaction made it impossible for her to suppress a smile.

"Where is he?" Baker asked.

"He doesn't come in until afternoon. He covered some game last night."

"Wake him up and get his ass in here."

Tish worked at her desk for more than an hour waiting for Carl Majors to arrive. She knew him only by his byline. She wasn't sure she'd ever laid eyes on him. The sports department was on the floor above the newsroom. They shared it with the online geeks who were transforming much of the news operation, making the webpage more robust. Word around the building was the online operation was financially carrying the rest of the organization.

The newspaper had done a complete financial turnaround in the past two years. Instead of layoffs, it had hired more than a hundred staffers for the news operation. Most of them were upstairs in the digital operation. She was among the handful of newbies in the newsroom on the second floor. All of them, she begrudged, had more experience than she.

She used the time to draw up a list of questions for Underwood. She wondered what he would say when they confronted him. Then a big shadow hovered over her desk and she looked up.

"Carl Majors," he said. "I understand you've asked me out on a date."

Tish played along. "I don't ask guys out on dates very often. I hope you understand how special this is." Nancy was right. Majors was a beast, and a damned good looking one. All muscle.

"Madam, you have made my day. You have saved me from the clutches of the nearest men's locker room permeating with odiferous spandex-clad barbarians—and that's just the coaching staff. Instead, you have offered me lilacs and beauty and the company of dirty politicians."

He'd noticed her perfume. No, he had noticed her. She enjoyed his flirtation. "I was told you were a soul in need of saving."

"That, my lady, would be impossible. It also assumes I have a soul." He cracked up and so did Tish. She stood and they shook hands. He was at least a foot taller than her.

She explained the situation and the likely chance the interview subject would become hostile. Carl didn't flinch.

The transition office was only four blocks away, so they decided to walk. As they walked down the sidewalk on K Street, Carl told her he was an Ohio State graduate who played football for two years before a knee injury ended his college football career and his scholarship. He apologized for coming in late. He had covered the Wizards game last night and it had gone into overtime. How boring, she thought.

Then he told her he had been an English major and loved Shakespeare. Tish gave herself an invisible slap in the psyche. She had prejudged him as a humorous dumb jock. She should have known better. Baker wouldn't hire someone unless they were really good at their job. As they stood on the corner of Fifteenth and K Streets waiting for the light to change, she realized his knuckles didn't drag on the sidewalk, and his conversation was as nimble as his apparent athletic ability.

She explained the video showing Underwood manipulating his cell phone at the time Crofton was shot. He said he understood his role was mainly bodyguard. Baker, he said, had told him it could be dangerous and asked him if he was willing to do this.

"This is purely voluntary on your part?" Tish asked.

"Well, he did say I would be with a very attractive woman. BB knows me well. He knew I wouldn't pass up a chance like this."

So, Carl had a thirst for risk, a sense of humor, and he was a complete flirt. She especially liked the latter. And he just gave her a better sense of her boss. Baker might come across as a gruff old man, but he was mentally ambidextrous at managing his newsroom. And he was very protective of his team as well. When everyone was attacking her story about the Senate investigating Templeton, Baker never questioned the integrity of her work.

She started feeling like she was part of a big family—one that was constantly under siege from the government and readers who didn't like what they published. And she was walking down the street with her first big brother.

"You know, if this doesn't go well, it won't be the end of the world," he said.

Was he seeing worry on her face?

"I've had a lot of locker room interviews that didn't go so well," he continued. "But then I talk to the coaches or trainers, and sooner or later, I get the whole story. There's always a way. Sometimes you just have to use a little ingenuity. I think nuance is key. I've always heard, 'You catch more flies with honey than vinegar.' I say nonsense. You catch more flies with nuance."

"Well, let's see how well we fly today."

Although I have to admit," he said, "when it comes to dumb jocks, honey might work just as well."

Tish smiled at him. His attempt to calm her down and cheer her up wasn't working, but it was kind of him to try. She couldn't escape it. Thinking about confronting Underwood raised her anxiety level.

They entered the non-descript building on K Street and took the elevator to the third-floor reception area. The rental furniture was cheap and the walls needed a paint job. It was obvious it had been rented in a hurry.

Tish identified herself and asked for Underwood. She feigned the most dispassionate tone she could muster and hoped her unease was not apparent. The receptionist told them to take a seat, and she called Underwood on her phone.

It was a full five minutes before he appeared, fully decked out in a suit and tie. He must have rushed to the restroom to put on his tie. Tish had seen no one wearing one since they arrived.

Underwood was handsome and had that Northeast establishment pretense about him, yet he seemed ecstatic to see two reporters interested in talking to him. He eagerly led them back to his office, talking all the while, explaining he was vetting candidates for high-level government jobs.

Age had tarnished what once must have been a law office. The expensive wood paneling was dull and scratched in places. Tish noticed piles of resumes on his desk among old coffee cups, his wallet and keys, and a cell phone. She wondered if it was the infamous cell phone.

He picked up some newspapers off two visitor chairs so they could sit, and gingerly placed the them on a teetering stack whose origins began somewhere in the base of a cardboard box marked for recycling. He apologized for the mess saying he'd worked late last night and the cleanup crew missed his office. Then he sat behind his desk, shoved a pile of papers to the side and leaned back in his chair.

Tish got right to the point.

"I don't know if you know I wrote the story that said the man the police had in custody for President-Elect Crofton's murder was the wrong man."

She watched his jaw gradually drop. He leaned forward, placing his hands in the empty space he had just created in front of him.

"The police determined someone inside the ballroom set off the weapon using the hotel's Wi-Fi," she continued. "The person manipulated the camera gun into position and fired it."

She watched his face, looking for any signs, as if he would suddenly give himself away. He didn't flinch. She was glad Carl was sitting in the chair next to her. Underwood seemed very cold.

She reached into her purse and pulled out a still of Underwood manipulating his phone on the stage on election night and handed it to him. "We have video of you at the precise time Crofton was shot. You were working an app on your cell phone. We know you manipulated the weapon and pulled the trigger signaling the weapon to kill Holly Crofton. You assassinated her."

Underwood's eyes bulged in a wild stare. "You're out of your mind. I did no such thing." Both hands, palms down, were now in a defensive position on his desk as if he were about to claw deep marks into the wood.

"The evidence is on the video. You can't deny it," Tish said. She turned to Carl. He nodded, looked very stern, and said nothing.

Underwood leaped to his feet. "You are fucking crazy. I thought you wanted to talk to me about the transition, and you're accusing me of murder. Get out of here." He flung his arm out, pointing toward the door.

She looked at Carl and neither of them moved.

"Get the fuck out of my office," Underwood screamed.

They still did not move.

Underwood walked over to his door and looked out into a large room filled with cubicles and then turned around and confronted them again. She could see some of the staff sitting in cubicles outside his door looking up toward the commotion.

"How dare you accuse me of such a thing. Now get out. Get out of here before I call the police," he said in a much softer voice.

Tish rose first. She was closest to the door. Underwood stepped back into the hallway to let her through. She took a few steps, waiting for Carl.

Underwood looked back into his office. "You too. Get the hell out of here."

Carl shrugged his shoulders and nonchalantly walked through the office door. He stopped right in front of Underwood, who was a good six inches shorter than Carl, and glared at him.

Tish had a feeling Carl had done this before. She immediately concluded the sports world was a lot tougher than she thought. Carl knew how to handle himself.

They walked to the reception area unaccompanied by Underwood. Tish did not look back. In the elevator when it was just the two of them, she sighed in despair.

"Well, that went well," she said.

Carl laughed. "You could say that."

"No," she said. "I'm being facetious."

"I thought you were trying to be ironic," Carl said. He looked at her with a wide grin.

"We didn't get anything. I didn't move the story forward at all."

The elevator doors opened, and they were soon on the sidewalk.

"I wouldn't say that," Carl said.

"And how do you reach that brilliant conclusion, Sherlock? He admitted to nothing."

They stopped at the intersection for the light to change.

"You did say he used his cell phone to fire the weapon. Yes?"

"Yeah. So?"

"Well, it would seem to me there was a perfectly good cell phone on his desk. Probably the murder weapon. Wouldn't you think?"

"Yes."

"Isn't that how cops solve their murder cases? They always look for the murder weapon. At least that's how it's done on television."

The light turned green, and the traffic roared passed them as they stepped into the street.

"And your point?" asked Tish.

"I noticed his cell phone is no longer on his desk."

"What do you mean it's no longer on his desk?"

"It slipped into my pocket."

"You didn't."

"Tell me you didn't forget already, Tish. Nuance. No honey involved. Just nuance."

"But how—"

"You distracted him for just a moment in the doorway."

"No. I mean how does this help us?"

"Oh jeez. You are a Neanderthal," he said. "You see, up in sports, away from your whirlwind political jungle down on the second floor, we commune daily with the online geeks who pay our salaries." They stepped back up onto the sidewalk and passed a sandwich shop with a special on Greek gyros. Tish looked at him and his reflection in the window, seeing both sides of him at once.

"In plain English," he said, "we sit across the room from network engineers, web designers, and social media black belts. They create the web pages that not only work on your home computer, but guess what else? Your cell phone as well."

Tish wondered where this was going.

"There's a guy across the room who set up my cell phone with all of the apps I need to cover sports. I can record interviews, check games in progress, watch close calls on video—I can do just about anything with my cell phone thanks to the geek gods on the third floor. One time when I lost an interview, Deacon, he's the Dude, showed me how to go back through my history on the cloud to retrieve it."

Tish was beginning to understand. "You mean?"

"Exactly. If this phone is the one he used to fire the weapon, the history is right here." Carl tapped his jacket pocket.

She leaped into Carl's arms hugging him until she realized how inappropriate she was being. She stepped back. "Uh sorry. I was, uh, well, uh, overcome." She looked down, completely embarrassed. In the middle of the sidewalk on a busy K Street, Tish had hugged a man she barely knew.

"Anytime you need a hug, I'm only one floor away," he said. "Me and the geek gods, we're just a few steps above your political infestation."

She felt gratitude. "You may have just saved my story." She reached up and touched his face. His smile was genuine. No humor this time to cover up a real connection.

When she stepped back, Carl bowed his head in a gentleman's exaggerated, almost mocking gesture of grace. "All in a day's work, my lady."

"Thank you. Thank you so much. So, you think your friend Deacon—"

"The dude."

"*The dude*, could find what's on this phone?"

"If it's there, he'll find it."

They were a block from the office, and Tish picked up her pace. Carl, whose legs were much longer than hers, easily kept up.

XXXV

When they stepped into the *Post-Examiner* building, they headed straight to the sports department. She'd never been on this floor before. She realized she needed to be more sociable and get around and meet more of the reporters in different departments. She had been so focused on her beat in her first months at the paper; she hadn't been a very friendly person.

Carl introduced her to Deacon, the Dude. No last name. He was short and fat, with a long beard and a comb-over. For the first time, she saw Carl pull the mystery phone out of his pocket. He explained to Deacon what he wanted.

"Password?" Deacon asked.

"No idea," said Carl.

"Okay, give me a few minutes. I've got to break into it first."

"I'll be at my desk," Carl said.

It was lunchtime, and the room was nearly empty except for a few editors watching sports talk shows on ESPN. Carl explained most reporters didn't show up until late afternoon if they were covering a game that night. The editors and columnists had regular hours, but they loved long lunches with each other to talk trash and sports.

He sat at his desk, and Tish sat at an empty desk next to his.

"That's Boz's desk," he said.

"Who?"

"Steve Bozwell, columnist extraordinaire."

"Who?"

"Really? You don't know the Boz?" Carl shook his head in mock disgust.

"Sorry. I don't read sports much."

"Maybe you should. He's won a Pulitzer. You know there's a lot more to this newspaper than politics."

"I'm beginning to understand that." She flashed him a wan smile.

Deacon interrupted. "It didn't take as long as I thought. The password was a piece of cake, and a quick search found this interesting site on the dark web." He laid the phone on Carl's desk. "Pull it up on your computer. It will be easier to see." Deacon told him how to get onto the dark web and gave him Underwood's account ID and the dark web URL.

He pointed at the screen as Tish huddled over Carl's shoulder.

"You see here," Deacon pointed at a dashboard on the screen. "And here are the remote controls to operate the weapon. Someone did a lot of work to create this site."

He clicked a button and a virtual joystick displayed. He moved it around with his cursor and it aimed a gun sight, much like a video game. He clicked on an icon on the gun sight and a still photo of Crofton appeared. He clicked on the photo and video of Crofton speaking lined up in the crosshairs. It ended before the weapon fired.

Here are the times he was last on this site," Deacon said, with no emotion in his voice.

Tish grabbed her reporter's notebook from her purse and copied the numbers. "Now, if I understand what you're looking for, you simply match these times to the time Crofton was shot. If they match, you've got your guy."

Tish knew the time by heart, and she scrolled through the dates and times on the screen. There it was. He had signed on three hours before Crofton had been shot and then signed off fifty minutes later. And then a half hour before Crofton had been assassinated, he'd signed on again. The numbers showed he'd signed off seconds after she'd been shot. He had never signed on again.

"Is there any possibility this could be wrong?" she asked. "What about time zones? Does this line up with the eastern time zone?"

"That's what you're looking at," Deacon said. "I made sure of that."

"And we're sure it's Underwood's phone?" She was covering all her bases. She couldn't believe how lucky she was.

"Right here." Deacon picked up the phone again off Carl's desk. "Right here on his phone is all of his information. It's a Verizon account. He purchased this phone thirteen months ago. I can go on and on."

"Okay. I'm convinced," said Tish. "Thanks, guys. I can take it from here."

"You might want a screenshot of the dark web site for your story," Carl suggested.

"Good idea."

XXXVI

Tish was back in Baker's office in five minutes. She explained to him and Nancy about the phone. She could see the excitement on their faces.

"The only thing is, Carl stole it. I'm uncomfortable with that, but had he not, we wouldn't have our story."

"You're going to have to confront Underwood before we go to press. You're going to have to tell him you found his phone."

"Found his phone?"

"Well, that's what happened, isn't it? Carl found his phone?"

She could see where this was leading. "I guess it is."

"After we've published, we need to turn it over to the FBI. It's evidence in the assassination of the president-elect of the United States. We can't play footsie on this one. No one needs to know how we discovered the phone, but when we determined its importance, we volunteered to turn it over to the government. You know anyone at the FBI we can give it to?"

"I do."

"Good. Then let's get the story out there and talk again after we've published. We'll figure out exactly how we'll turn it over to the FBI." Baker shook his head. "Damn. How do you keep doing this? Over and over again, you keep coming up with these huge stories. Now I've got to go thank Meryl for kicking me in the ass and telling me what an asset you'd be to National. That woman deserves a bottle of champagne."

He turned to Nancy. "You've got a good one here," he said.

She smiled. "Couldn't agree more."

The lovefest was over. She got it now. Loved one second, scorned the next. She must always be on her toes.

Tish returned to her desk and began to write. She had four hours to pull the story together, but she had it done in one.

All she had left was a phone call to Underwood. She called the transition office main number. She was surprised he picked up his extension.

"You stole my phone," he yelled.

"I did not."

"I want it back."

"Care to comment on why you were on a secret dark website hooked up to that camera-weapon at the precise time it fired and killed Holly Crofton?"

"You rot in hell," he said, and she heard his desk phone slam down in her ear. She quoted him verbatim in her story.

Nancy read the piece and suggested several changes. Nothing Tish couldn't live with. She pulled up Tom's original video on her computer, most of which they had not used, and found the portion with Underwood standing on stage looking intently at his phone. However, she quickly realized his footage did not show Underwood at the precise moment Crofton had been shot. Tom's camera was focused on Crofton. And when the weapon had exploded, Tom's camera had rocked upward toward the ceiling and tilted sideways. He had been shaken by the concussion of the explosion next to him. So Nancy asked the online desk if they could purchase any other video of the stage that night.

The call from upstairs came swiftly. Another cameraman had a distant view of the entire stage just as Crofton was shot. They were able to zoom in and enhance the area where Underwood had stood and it showed a grainy picture of him tapping his finger on his cell phone a second before the explosion. Everyone on the stage had jumped, and a quiet sudden shock ensued for a few seconds, followed by bedlam. All the while, Underwood was still texting.

"Perfect," Nancy said. "Get that ready for the web and give me a series of stills for the print version."

By the time of their afternoon news meeting at four o'clock, Nancy had put an entire package together that also included Underwood's photo and bio. Tish could see the editors all meeting inside their glass-enclosed conference room along with Robey. Baker sat at the head of the table. Each editor had a lineup of stories to pitch for the front page, but Tish had no doubt where hers would be.

She didn't start to leave until six-thirty, after Nancy had assured her everything was fine. Robey had approved her story and Baker was still there but had changed into a tux. He was going to some political function tonight or one of those Georgetown parties, Tish suspected. He walked by her desk as she was preparing to leave.

"Nice work, Tish. Keep it up. You may be the least experienced on the National Desk, but you've proven you belong here." He pivoted and left. She watched his tall lean frame meander toward the elevator, and stop, briefly, to talk to two other reporters. He carried himself with a swagger of confidence. She wanted to be just like that.

She sat at her desk enjoying the moment. She realized for the first time Baker had called her by name. Did that mean anything? Yeah, it did. She had arrived.

SHE GRABBED TOM AS SOON as she got home and hugged him for a long time. This time she was hugging the right guy. Exhausted, they both collapsed on the couch to watch the news and eat leftover pizza.

Tish wondered when they would release her story on the web and then her phone rang.

"Grant here. I just heard. Good work."

"How did you find out?"

"It was just on CNN."

Shit, she thought. They were watching the wrong network.

"Tom, quick, flip it to CNN," she yelled and then realized what she had done to Grant's hearing. "Sorry, Jim," she said in a much softer voice.

Tom caught it in mid-story. CNN was showing the video as several talking heads discussed it. Tish watched, first ignoring Grant on the line and then she returned to her conversation. "Jim, thanks. I was watching the wrong channel."

"Don't worry. They'll all have it shortly. Your story is the biggest thing since the Kennedy assassination. The difference is, we have no doubt who the assassin is this time thanks to you. Good work." He said goodbye and hung up.

Tish felt a tingle all over her body. She was proud of her work. Her only concern was how Carl had obtained the phone now locked in Nancy's desk in a plastic baggie, ready for the FBI. She had agreed with Baker that even though they obtained the phone under questionable circumstances, they couldn't be constrained by that. The story was just too important. Professional ethics, she was learning, yielded to the circumstances sometimes.

XXXVII

She was again in the office early, before most other reporters and before the desk editors arrived. Tish used the time to reread the print version of the *Post-Examiner* and grab a couple of extra copies to take home later. She'd never had a banner headline on the front page. It was mesmerizing. Six columns all the way across the top of the page. Wow. That was as big as it got.

She went online to look at other news organizations' accounts of her work and tuned into several cable news channels to see what they were saying this morning.

The cable channels were now parked outside Underwood's apartment building, reporting live. They found no answer at his door. A neighbor said he had gone out last night and she had not seen him return.

Tish wondered if he had fled. If she were in his shoes, she probably would.

Nancy arrived and came by her desk. "Everything is looking good. I'll talk to Baker this morning and then I think we need to make a call to the FBI."

Tish agreed.

Twenty minutes later she saw Nancy in Baker's office and a short time after she was standing at Tish's desk again.

"Baker wants to wait until the morning editors' meeting. He just wants to inform them of what we are doing and get their feedback. He's off to tell the publisher right now."

Tish hadn't thought about how much was involved and how many people it took to see her story through to the end. She was beginning to appreciate that things were done a lot differently at a big city newspaper.

Tish called Grant and invited him to lunch or coffee. She wanted to kill a few hours before the editors' meeting and maybe pick up some gossip and reaction to her story.

"Can't do it today," he said. "Sorry. How 'bout tomorrow?"

She agreed.

She was going stir-crazy. Maybe some outdoor exercise. When she left the building, she discovered a cool blustery day. She crossed the street to McPherson Square. An old lady was feeding pigeons, and a heap of scratchy blue blankets, which she recognized as a homeless person, was sleeping on a park bench. She thought it unusual. Most homeless slept on the heating grates to keep warm.

She sat on a bench across the park path from the pigeon lady and thought about how her career had burst forward in almost record time. She needed to consider how to handle this sudden fame, and how it might affect her life. She'd already been called once about appearing on television, and she had turned it down. Had she made the right move? She needed Nancy's advice. She couldn't do this alone. She liked the support of a powerful newspaper.

An old woman passed by and asked her for a quarter. Tish had always ignored the homeless. She pitied them and always kept her distance. They scared her. There, but for the grace of God, she thought.

She needed to move beyond her bubble. She reached into her purse and pulled out a five-dollar bill and handed it to the old woman. The woman stared at the money in disbelief.

"Bless you," she said. She quickly tucked it in her baggy clothing and walked on, looking furtively from side to side as if someone might steal her newfound riches.

Tish wondered if the old woman would use it to buy alcohol or food. Her priest had warned her about giving the homeless money.

She decided she wasn't going to judge. She had touched someone's life. That's all that mattered.

BAKER CAME OUT OF THE EDITORS' MEETING at precisely eleven thirty and strolled over to Tish's desk. "Make your phone call," he said. "Everyone is on board from the publisher on down to the entire editorial team. Who are you calling?"

"Joel Kopperud has been my source inside the FBI. I thought I'd call him."

"Do it," he said. He walked off.

Tish reached Kopperud on his cell phone on the third ring. He immediately agreed to meet her. She figured she was now the new hot commodity in town. Washington mirrored Hollywood in its lust for celebrity.

XXXVIII

Tish invited Kopperud to a small café south of Alexandria on US Route 1. She had first heard of it from Beck Rikki, the newspaper's former star investigative reporter. They'd met by accident one day in the company cafeteria while he was waiting to meet an old friend. She'd immediately recognized him and confided in him her goals as a journalist. She wanted to be like him and explained she needed a discreet place to talk to sources. He'd smiled and offered up this place, saying it had served him well. No one in the political establishment, he assured her, would ever show their face in this place.

Now she understood why. It was shabby but clean. She wondered if she could trust the food. But Rikki had said the food wasn't bad and was an eclectic mix of the Americas—everything from cheeseburgers and Reubens, to enchiladas and fajitas.

She spotted Kopperud already seated, drinking a cup of tea. She sat down across from him in a rickety metal chair, and he explained he had a sore throat. Normally, he said, by now he would be guzzling his fifth cup of coffee.

"I have a present for you," she said.

"I was hoping you would."

She slid the phone encased in its plastic baggie over to his side. He picked it up almost nonchalantly, looked at it, turned it over, and pocketed it."

"How'd you get it?"

"I can't say."

"Figured."

"I feel badly. I feel like we should have given you a heads-up earlier about Underwood. I fear he's escaped already."

"Oh, don't worry about him. White-collar criminals have no idea how to cover their tracks. He withdrew all of his cash from his savings and checking accounts right at nine this morning when the bank opened. He knew enough not to use his credit cards. Anybody with a brain knows we can trace you in seconds doing that. But he forgot about his commuter EZ Pass to pay highway tolls. It's attached to his windshield, giving us plenty of information. We've been tracking him for hours. We know exactly where he is. Your newspaper will be reporting tomorrow that we picked him up in Lynchburg, Virginia. He traveled down Interstate Ninety-Five to Richmond and then headed southwest."

"Wow. That didn't take any time."

"We know what we're doing."

"Well, the newspaper wanted to make sure you had the phone," said Tish. "Everything I wrote about is right there on this contraption."

"We appreciate it. You know, the FBI has a long, difficult history with the press. It's nice when we can work together, although we both know our roles conflict a lot of the time."

"Most of the time," said Tish.

She smiled at him and he smiled back.

"We can't always tell you what you want to know. We just can't. But it would be nice if we could work together when our interests merge."

Tish understood what he was alluding to. "Maybe even become friends one day."

"That wouldn't hurt either one of us."

Kopperud appeared to be in his late thirties and on his way up in the bureau. They were both going in the same direction. Someday, they may need each other again.

"I'd like to think I could call you and what I said remained just between us," said Tish.

"Exactly what I was thinking," said Kopperud.

He took a swig of his tea, stood up and laid a five-dollar bill on the table. "Good luck," he said.

She turned and watched him walk quickly out of the restaurant and disappear.

XXXIX

Kopperud was right. The next morning the *Post-Examiner* carried the arrest of Buckley Underwood. Tish felt a sense of relief as she sat in the newsroom and read the story. She knew she had put to rest part of this crazy affair, but she also knew she wasn't finished.

She was glad Tom had refused to tell the authorities about the Russians. She, like him, had come to mistrust the motives of some government officials. She wasn't sure whom to trust. But she certainly got the impression from her conversations the Templeton people were to be taken deadly seriously. "Deadly," being the key word, if she were to believe Grant. And he was one of the few she could trust.

What she didn't understand was how the Russians were involved in the plot to kill Holly Crofton. Somehow, it appeared they must have been working with Buckley Underwood. She had a recording that appeared to be as good as a confession.

What was their connection?

Who was in the mystery van shown in the video outside the hotel? Did the New York police have the right guy? And who was smart enough to build that weapon that killed Crofton? It sure wasn't Underwood.

It had to be a conspiracy. Crofton's murder involved several people. Good God. Had she become one of those people—a loony conspiracy theorist? People would soon start thinking she talked to herself. She could just envision herself in a tinfoil hat.

She needed to get serious. She wasn't done. So many questions remained unanswered.

XL

They were meeting at a café in upper Northwest Washington near the Maryland line. Grant had called an hour earlier saying he had a last-minute appointment in the city and wouldn't have time to drive to the Virginia suburbs where Tish had suggested they meet. Tish took a cab. No Metro stations were nearby.

Grant was sitting at a table with a beer and plate of pickles in front of him when she arrived. She grinned. No mustard this time. He fidgeted in his chair as she sat down. A glass of red wine was waiting for her on the table.

She eyed it, and him, questioning. He nodded.

"Congratulations. Well done." Grant lifted his beer glass, and waited for her. They clinked in celebration.

"Thanks. It's been one of the most unreal experiences of my life," Tish said.

She looked closely at him. Something was bothering him. "What's wrong?"

"I'm worried about you." He chomped on his pickle. "People in Templeton's path don't end up well. You've stepped into some pretty deep shit."

"Oh, I'm not worried about Underwood," Tish said. She was beginning to think he was being a bit overly dramatic.

"That's not what I'm talking about. I'm talking about your story about Templeton's mental health." He wiped his mouth with a cloth napkin.

"What do you mean?"

"Leigh is dead," he said.

Tish gasped.

"The police found her this morning in her hotel room five blocks from the White House. Her throat was slit. She was beaten so badly they couldn't recognize her."

He exhaled a long sigh and looked down.

"They had to identify her from her driver's license and belongings in the room. I was told she put up a hell of a fight. There was blood everywhere." He shook his head, still looking down at the table. "That's why I couldn't meet in Virginia today. I'm meeting an acquaintance in emergency services in an hour who promised more details."

Tish felt the air go out of her lungs. "I'm so sorry. Can I do anything?" It was inadequate, she knew, but it was all she could muster. "That's just so unbelievable."

"You may have gotten into more trouble than you bargained for." Grant placed his arms on the table in front of him and looked her in the eye. "Just watch yourself. They must have figured out Leigh was your source. You must act as if they did. They had no reason to kill her unless they thought she was a threat to Templeton."

"Who are *they*?" Tish asked.

"Don't know exactly. But they obviously want Templeton in power." He calmly grabbed another pickle and crunched down on it.

"You can prove this?"

"Of course not."

"I'm sorry. I feel responsible." His words were beginning to sink in.

"Don't. You're not. It had to be Templeton's people. I'd bet he knows exactly who did it."

"Why do you say that?" Tish wondered if Grant might be too close to the situation. His friend was dead. He was distraught. Tish got that. But the thought that Templeton ordered Leigh Child's murder was ludicrous. The real political world didn't operate that way. Washington insiders may be corrupt and power hungry, but they're not crazy.

"Underwood," Grant said. "Remember, he worked for Templeton. He was Templeton's eyes and ears on Crofton's side of the campaign."

"Really? They do that?"

"What was Leigh doing for us?"

"Oh, yeah."

"In politics, people are always watching what they say because they don't know who the person sitting across the table from them really is—where their loyalties truly lie." Grant took a swig of his beer and set the glass back down. "And don't forget, Templeton comes from the rough and tumble of New York real estate. He's rubbed shoulders with the Mafia since he was in diapers. He's one tough mother. Look, you've done well coming out of the starting gate, but you're too close to the ground. You gotta look up sometimes."

Tish understood.

"Think about it a minute," he continued. "As soon as Templeton was elected vice president, Crofton suddenly became the one obstacle in his path to the pinnacle. What blows my mind is that it was as if he had anticipated their win all along. But he couldn't have. Nobody could. It was a friggin' miracle—a perfect storm. Yet her assassination took a lot of planning and—" Grant stopped, his mouth open. He cocked his head and looked into the distance at nothing.

Tish could tell he had figured out something.

"What?" Tish shouted, almost jumping out of her seat. "What?" she said softly, conscious of her outburst.

"It couldn't have been a decision based on their win." He looked at her and shook his head. "The plan was too elaborate, too complicated. I mean how long did it take to build that gun that looked like a camera? Yeah, it took planning."

"Yes?" Tish prodded.

"Don't you see? That means win or lose, Crofton was going to be assassinated."

Tish leaned in on the table. She was going crazy trying to make sense of Grant's logic.

"What?" Tish could almost see the wheels turning in his head.

"Who figures to benefit from Crofton's death?" he lowered his voice in a conspiratorial tone.

"Templeton?"

"Exactly. Her death put Templeton in line to become the party's nominee in four years. So, no matter what, Crofton was a dead woman."

Tish picked up the thread. "Wait a minute. If she had lost, wouldn't that have automatically given Templeton the advantage of winning the party nomination in four years? I don't see the logic. Why did he need to kill her if she was no longer in his way?"

"Crofton's people held the reins to the party machinery, and she hated Templeton. Oh, she was cynical enough to use him for her own purposes—use his financial connections to fund her campaign. But she would have done anything to keep him from getting the nomination four years hence. No doubt he understood that. Theirs was an allegiance of convenience. Nothing more."

"So he was going to have her killed, win or lose?"

"And even if Templeton didn't order her assassination, someone in his camp did. Someone who wanted him in office as badly as he wanted the job. That means there was someone out there—loyalists or well-funded supporters working behind the scenes—doing whatever necessary to ensure he became president."

"But why? What was their motivation?"

"I don't know. It was something worth killing for. Don't kid yourself, Tish. You're now up against some powerful folk. In their positions, they will have access to levers of power you've never dreamed of. It will be just you and your notebook and that newspaper of yours against the world."

"That newspaper is pretty powerful," Tish said. "I've certainly learned that over the past few weeks."

"Even so, you're expendable. You need to watch your back," Grant said. He looked down at the table and his lonely beer. "You're big time now. Crofton and now Child are both dead. So who's next? Who is

Derrick Templeton's biggest threat right now? Who most stands in his way?"

He looked her straight in the eye. "We're talking about the soon-to-be most powerful man in the world. And who are you? A kid reporter with a notepad."

Tish thought about where she'd come from and what she had accomplished in such a short period. She remembered all of the lessons learned and how she had struggled to fit in with her new, fast-paced environment. She hadn't dressed right. She hadn't asked the right questions. She was fumbling her way through the process.

Yet her editors had seemed to overlook all of that. It was as if they mistook her for a child prodigy when she knew she was just plain lucky. She had naively taken advantage of an opportunity and was in the middle of riding the wave before she even realized it. What happens when she finally falls off? They would see right through her.

"I want to be very clear," Grant said. "You need to give this up. It's too dangerous."

"I'm not done," she said. "There's more to this. Others, as you say, were involved. Who was in the van on the videotape? And why were the police so set on accusing the wrong man—a man they still will not identify—when all they had to do was look at the people standing on the stage near Crofton? It wasn't rocket science figuring that one out. I think someone in a position of power didn't want the truth to come out about Buckley Underwood. But who?

"And what about the Russians? I haven't told anyone, but Tom recorded two of them in the ballroom on election night, and their conversation made clear they were involved. It was as good as a confession."

Grant looked stunned. "What?"

"Yes. So, you see, I have to continue."

"What did the Russians say?"

"They alluded to the man in the truck outside."

Grant fidgeted in his chair again and took another gulp of beer. "Please walk away."

"It's what I do," Tish said. And for the first time, she did look up from the ground. She knew exactly where she stood and it felt good.

Grant looked irritated. He took a swig of beer and checked his phone for text messages.

"Shit. Excuse me just a second. I need to text this guy back." When he was done, he placed his phone on the table. "Sorry, my meeting has been moved up and I need to take a quick call. I guess we're done. You're moving forward. I can't convince you to stop. Please watch yourself."

She appreciated his concern. It was somehow endearing.

"You take off first. I need to catch this call before I leave," Grant said. "I don't think we should be seen walking out of here together, and I wouldn't mind finishing my beer." He grinned and nodded his head in recognition of his half-empty draft on the table.

Wow, he hadn't finished a single beer, Tish realized. How many had he drunk at their first meeting? Three? Four? Maybe he'd finish those god-awful pickles too. Tish grabbed her purse and opened her wallet.

"Don't bother," he said. "I think I can handle a glass of wine."

She smiled at his small kindness, said goodbye, and left. As she stepped through the door to a cold gray day, she turned around and looked at Grant. He was looking at his cell phone. She thought about how grateful she was she had made that first call to him and set up their initial meeting. She understood he was helping her for his own selfish reasons, but that's what sources do. She couldn't argue with the results and their effect on her life and career.

She turned toward the street and hailed the first cab she saw. She hopped in and gave the driver her address. The driver slammed on the gas too hard, jerking the car and knocking her back in the seat as they sped away.

"Hey," she said, "slow down please."

After adjusting herself in the back seat, she looked up at the driver in the rearview mirror. Their eyes met. He smiled, and she recognized him immediately. He was one of the Russians who impersonated the FBI.

"Stop this car," she screamed. Tish reached for the door handle and heard the locks click. The handle didn't move. She tried the window. It didn't open. She pounded on the clear plastic partition between her and the driver as the cab raced down the street. "Let me out of here!"

THE DRIVER HELD THE WHEEL and grinned as the young woman pummeled the plastic shield separating them. The battering stopped and he watched her through his mirror as she fruitlessly struggled to open the rear door. He controlled all of the car's locks and windows from his armrest on the driver's door.

He raced through a red light amid a blast of car horns and swerved to miss an oncoming truck. He drove with one hand with the ease of the professional driver he once was, weaving in and out between cars as he raced toward the beltway. He picked up his cell phone lying on the passenger seat next to him and pressed automatic dial.

It rang twice and a familiar voice picked up.

"Grant here."

End of Part One

Read an excerpt from Rick Pullen's best-selling novel

Naked Ambition

I

With his secret secure and brain afire, Beck was alive. Fueled by a rush of adrenalin, his mind would not rest. But it was not always that way. Like now. Oh man, especially like now.

Grateful to finally be home in the solace of his cluttered condominium after a turbulent morning flight back to Washington, Beck was cranking through a chilling novel and a second Corona Light. He'd suffered through five interminable days in a fleabag in Flyover, America. And for what? The stale beer? The stench of cigarettes? No, it was the lumpy bed and the low-pitched rumble of the sputtering air conditioner. Or maybe the all-night, rag-tag symphony of truckers braking at the intersection just outside his hotel. Yeah. That was it. Had to be. The price of admission to his world.

His cell phone rang. Not now, he thought.

He'd just reached the climax, where the hero discovered his beautiful accomplice was an enemy spy. Finally, Beck would learn...

The damn thing rang again.

He glared at it, vibrating on his coffee table, willing it to shut up and stop dancing.

Caller ID was blocked. Shit. He looked back at the page, determined to finish the chapter, but his eyes refused to focus. His DNA was nothing if not emphatic. God, he hated that about himself.

"Yeah?" he grumbled into the phone.

"Beck Rikki?"

"Yeah."

"The reporter for the *Post-Examiner*?"

"Maybe. Who's calling?"

"Daniel Fahy, head of the Public Integrity Section at Justice. Your office said I could reach you at this number. I'd like to speak with you privately."

"About?"

"I'd rather not say over the phone. Can we meet?"

Not another crackpot, thought Beck. He'd just finished a week of hounding false leads. He didn't need this right now. "Got a thing about phones?"

"It would be more appropriate to discuss what I have to say face-to-face."

"How do I know that?"

"You'll just have to trust me."

"Why should I? I haven't a clue who you are."

"I just told you."

Beck groaned softly. He needed to talk to the City Desk about giving out his number. "Look, I've had a bad week. Lost my appetite for wild goose chase. Throw me a bone."

"Are you always this difficult?"

"Occupational hazard. You always this secretive?"

"Occupational hazard."

Beck leaned back on his couch and stared at the ceiling, waiting. Not another smartass government bureaucrat whining about his boss mistreating him. Why do these loons always call a reporter instead of HR?

Fahy fell silent, but Beck heard muffled laughter in the background. "You still there?"

"I'm thinking," Fahy said.

Beck heard more laughter. "That's okay. While you're at your party, I'm sitting here quietly engrossed in one of the best novels I've read all year. I've got nothing better to do with my time than to listen to silence on *my* end of *your* phone call."

"Okay. Okay. I think I've run across a bribery scheme involving a very important public official—a *very important* public official. Interested?"

Beck sat up straight. "I could be. How important is important?"

"Near the top of the Washington food chain."

"Meaning?"

"He looks in the mirror every morning and imagines he sees the President."

"That's half of Washington."

"He's already taken the measurements of the Oval Office and ordered new carpet."

Beck felt his brain spark. It was like striking a match. Then just as quickly, the familiar refrain of his defenses jumped in to douse the flames.

"Why tell me?" he asked. "I thought you Justice guys liked to do this sort of investigation in the shadows. You hate the press."

"I've got my reasons. I'll make you a deal. I'll not only give you what I think is a story, but I'll explain my motivation for calling you when we meet. Fair enough?"

"Not fair, but it's enough." Beck had to play ball. He'd just about gone crazy over the past several months. It had been too long since he published a significant investigative piece. His editors had been hounding him. One even suggested he be assigned to a regular beat again. A beat? For the most decorated investigative reporter at the paper? How humiliating.

Fahy suggested breakfast the next day and gave Beck directions to a restaurant south of Old Town Alexandria on old US Route 1, a good ten miles outside of Washington.

"How will I recognize you?"

"Don't worry," Fahy said. "You will." And hung up.

To read more, purchase online at Amazon.com.

COMING IN 2018

Another Beck Rikki thriller, *Naked Truth,* the sequel to *Naked Ambition.*

About the Author

Rick Pullen has spent his career as an investigative reporter and magazine editor. Although the subjects of his numerous investigative pieces have sometimes accused him of writing fiction, he actually never attempted until 2011. His first novel, *Naked Ambition*, was published in 2016 and became an instant Amazon bestseller. He now has several book projects underway. *Naked Truth*, a sequel to *Naked Ambition*, is scheduled for publication in 2018.

In 2015 Rick was named to the *Folio 100*—the 100 most influential people in magazine publishing. The same year he was a finalist for editor of the year.

To learn more about Rick and his books, visit his website at www.RickPullen.com.

9 780999 491003